STAR WARRIORS

"My guild-lord Brodok?"

His eyes glanced up at me, hunted and full of
fear. He was sitting on a long couch from which
the stuffing protruded. He wore his grey nightshirt, and it was rumpled round his knees. His
long white fleshy legs were angled like the arms of
some strange catapult.

"Has someone harmed you?"

"No one has harmed me, Cal."

"The Star?"

"The Star has gone – all hope has been destroyed."
My lord gazed into my eyes with a look I'd never
seen: a look of hopelessness.

Also in the Point Fantasy series:

POINT FANTASY

STAR WARRIORS

Peter Beere

Cover illustration by David Wyatt

SCHOLASTIC

Scholastic Children's Books
Scholastic Publications Ltd,
7–9 Pratt Street, London NW1 0AE, UK

Scholastic Inc.,
555 Broadway, New York, NY 10012-3999, USA

Scholastic Canada Ltd,
123 Newkirk Road, Richmond Hill,
Ontario, Canada L4C 3G5

Ashton Scholastic Pty Ltd,
P O Box 579, Gosford, New South Wales,
Australia

Ashton Scholastic Ltd,
Private Bag 92801, Penrose, Auckland,
New Zealand

First published by Scholastic Publications Ltd, 1995

Copyright © Peter Beere, 1995

Cover illustration copyright © David Wyatt, 1995

ISBN 0 590 55706 8

Typeset by TW Typesetting, Midsomer Norton, Avon

Printed by Cox & Wyman Ltd, Reading, Berks.

10 9 8 7 6 5 4 3 2 1

PROLOGUE

A band of riders came from the twilight at a steady canter, heading northwards towards the Field of Blood where my grandfather fell in the last days of the War. He died saving his wife from a pack of gore-flecked wolves, and she followed him soon after. It was grief, I think, that caused her death, or maybe fear – fear that the Dark Land hordes would overrun the earth. For a time it had looked as though they would, so I have been told, for few remained to drive them from our land. Most of our fighters had been captured or slaughtered or had fled, and only when the Star crashed to the earth were our foes forced to turn back. The Star came to our aid by bringing blindness down to confuse Gaylor's horde. Of course this is all history, and long before my *time; all that I really know are the twisted tales and legends that have been handed down. But when the riders came that day they made me quake inside, and turned my thoughts to war ...*

I did not want to burn in a blaze of Gaylor's fire; I did not want to die. Throughout my childhood his name had haunted me: the Hunter of the Night, the Bringer of the Dark, the half-mage warrior who rose up from the ruins of Kethelmodolok. In far distant times that nation had waged a bitter war against the eastern kings and the very world itself had been brought to the brink of destruction. Nothing was left standing by the time the smoke had cleared. No landscape was left untouched by the carnage which was wrought. Nobody claimed the field, for no one had the strength to hoist their banner. It was a slaughter from which no side emerged either victorious or without lasting scars. No force emerged with pride; no prize was claimed at all. Each side lost everything.

In the resulting mayhem, as warriors returned to their homes to rebuild their shattered lives and pray for their murdered kin, Lord Gaylor took his force – such of it as still remained – into the Underworld. This dark and strange realm lies underneath our own: a mirror for the earth but painted black. Here Gaylor forged a pact with the Lords who ruled that land, and then betrayed them. He overthrew them and hoisted his own flag. He took their seat of power and claimed it for his own. He pulled their great halls down and from their shattered stones raised up his Death Palace. Then he waited, quiescent, still and dark. He made his awful plans for ruling the whole earth. He reached into the soul of Night itself, and plucked the flame from it.

At last Death rose up through caverns, cracks and wells, and again war raged on earth. One by one the warriors fell and their new cities were torn down, and whole nations were enslaved.

This was the Great War, which lasted many years, though this time we were weak, while Gaylor had grown strong. He had a new ally in the darkness of the night which billowed in his wake.

In the final conflict on the Field of Blood, Lord Gaylor slew the last of those who survived. There my own grandparents fell, and Moridor itself lay open to his charge. Across the Great Plain which lies far to the north the remnants fled in droves before Lord Gaylor's force. They cast their weapons down, but he cut them through as though they were but chaff.

Gaylor was triumphant, and Darkness filled the sky as smoke poured from the fires he had lit within the earth. He dimmed the sun and moon; he banned the starlight. Lord Gaylor reigned supreme.

Then the Star came, plummeting down to earth. Some say it was a gift thrown down by God as a last hope for mankind. So intense was the new Star's light that those from Gaylor's caves were driven back by it.

Then the city of Moridor claimed the Star and hid it in a vault, and now it feeds us light and keeps us safe from harm. But we know Gaylor waits, working on evil schemes which will destroy our Star …

PART 1

CHAPTER 1

"Callibar?"

"Yes, my lord?"

"Did you leave the city today? Answer me honestly."

I let my head hang as I murmured, "Yes, Brodok."

"You know the law," he said. "Why do you flout it so?"

"I'm curious," I replied. "I went to see the place where my ancestors died. They were my family."

"We are your family now."

I nodded.

"Am I not like a father to you?"

I nodded again. Yes, he was. The only kin I had was my guild-lord Brodok-Dol.

"This strange obsession that you have for delving in the past – your room of souvenirs, your relics from the War—"

"The War frightens me, Lord."

"The War is dead and gone."

"It may come back again."

This is the constant nightmare I have – I am scared of war. I am scared of Gaylor's power, and the threat of endless dark. I am scared of growing up as one of Gaylor's slaves, serving his twisted thoughts. However, Brodok is not as scared as me. Brodok is chained to his bed, and that occupies his thoughts. My lord is a Star-Adept, and the fate which awaits Adepts is pain and madness. They cannot prevent it, for the Star sears through their brains, despite the masks and shields they wear when handling it. It is a great honour to be close to the Star, but the toll is a heavy one.

My lord rattled at his chains and mumbled, "On the plain – what do you see out there?"

"Nothing," I said, "except the plain and dust. Though today I saw a force of riders from the east. They swung round to the north—"

"The north? Some riders there?" (This seemed to interest him.)

"Yes, Lord," I murmured. "Riders on jet-black steeds."

"They did not challenge you?"

"They did not see me, Lord."

"Curious," Brodok said, as he battled clumsily to sit up on his bed. My lord is simple-minded and likes to ponder things which have no place at all in the schemes which rule the world. The hours spent with the Star have eaten through his brain, carving holes in his thoughts.

"I had a sword once, but I think I threw it away. Or maybe it was changed for something less bizarre. We have no need of swords, we Star-Adepts—"

"Yes, Lord," I muttered back.

I cleaned Lord Brodok's room while he sat on his bed murmuring incoherently. It pains me to see him drift away into the insane thoughts caused by exposure to the Star. The point he has reached now is just a staging post in his remorseless decline. Eventually he will reach such depths of insanity that he will be locked away in one of the padded cells where Adepts wait to die. Our Star is a mighty bride, and privilege and rank count for nought in the end. It is the paradox of our exalted guild that while we supply the light which keeps our city bright, we are all doomed to die in a darkness so intense few can conceive of it.

"Have we some water?"

"No, Lord, the water has gone." (It is in such short supply we have to trade for it.) "I shall get some more tomorrow."

Brodok slumped back on his bed. "I suffer such a thirst …"

Of course, I'm some way short of being a Star-Adept – a million miles or more. I'll never make it, for I am not of noble birth; I am an orphan child adopted by the guild. Though I am 'senior' now I'll never rise to more than glorified room-boy. I shall keep on serving my master till he dies, then they'll find someone else for me to feed and bathe. I'll keep watching the Star punch holes through my lords' brains until they age and die, but at least I shan't go mad. I shan't feel health and life drain slowly through my pores. I'll never feel the heat of Starlight through those masks my lords are forced to wear. I'll just keep polishing the lead until it shines, hoping to turn the rays so that they will live one more day. The masks are so ornate, so heavy, so complex – but still the Star shines through …

"Callibar?"

"Yes, my Lord?"

"On the day that I go mad, release me from my chains."

I stilled my sweeping. (I was still cleaning his

room.) "I cannot do that, Lord; it goes against the rules."

"I know, but some do it. Lord Guffdor was unchained and ran off through the halls."

"But the guards killed him—"

"That's the point," my guild-lord said. "He did not have to die locked in a padded cell. He suffered one quick thrust and his torment came to an end."

"And his slave was put to death."

"But I'll leave you a note, Cal, absolving you from blame. I'll say I *ordered* you, and you can't go against a command."

"You are asking me to kill a man whom I have grown to love."

"Love does such terrible things ..."

Chapter 2

I went into the town to find a special treat for my guild-lord Brodok. He is such a good man – unlike, say, Lord Gravlok, who takes an obscene delight in beating up his slaves, and is a bloated whale scarcely able to move, except to feed some more. Brodok, by comparison, is gentle and mild by temperament, and though his massive bulk is doubtless filled with power he has a feline grace, a delicacy of touch, and a softness of tongue. I have heard him singing when he thought he was alone, and he could charm the larks from the city's walls. I was fortunate that he adopted me to be his boy-servant. If I had been less charmed I might have got Gravlok, who now collared me as I walked through the doors. He wanted artichokes and chickens from the town. Such chores could take all day.

We don't have much choice of food now, for the fields around the town are dry and desolate. Life is harder than it was some years ago, for the constant Dark Land threat saps the townspeople's will. The endless, swirling smoke which has replaced the sky's rain clouds depresses us all. The spirit has died in us, and I think that's why Gaylor waits; he is choking us by degrees. His hordes could probably destroy Moridor at a stroke. Our army is tired and weak and seems to lack the will to engage in a war. We have the Star, of course, but I don't think Gaylor's men would let themselves be caught by blindness for a second time. I think he is waiting, taunting us, saving us for the last.

The city of Moridor bustles as only cities can – grey streets filled with people in greyer clothes. Footpads and war-veterans jostle with fat merchants riding on snow-white steeds with tall plumes on their heads. Rich mansions overlook the poor quarters where refuse crawls and reeks. We've all been crammed in now behind high stone walls, and the farms which lay outside have been plundered and razed. People from miles around battle for living space, and our town is barely coping. There's so little to go round, so little air to breathe, so little room to move. One day we'll be so packed we won't be able to turn; we'll be one solid mass.

While I was scouring the stalls which crowd the market-place a friend of mine approached. His name is Flaymonar and he's a clay-fetcher for the Guild of Brickmakers and Likewise Allied Trades. He has long golden hair, which would be worth a lot to the Guild of Wigmakers. We have a lot of guilds; in fact, we're all in guilds. We even have a guild for those who are guildless. In the town of Moridor, we each have a place.

"Cal, have you heard the news? The Sacred Stone is cracked—"

"That's just a rumour," I replied.

Flaymonar grabbed my left arm, which was reaching out to steal a brooch as a present for Brodok. (I have no money left.) "This one is real," he insisted. "It's not the Rumourers – it's from the Guild of Truth."

"Yes, yes, I've heard it," I muttered irritably. (As I've said, everyone is irritable these days.) "And they've been saying the same since the day we were born. We're all still here, aren't we?"

"What if it's true, though?"

"It won't be, Flay," I said. "It never was before, so why should it be this time? The Sacred Stone is

14

safe, nothing can break it down."

"Dark magic could," he said. Dark magic … Gaylor's spells, conjured up by scientists aided by their black mages.

"What do you think will happen, if they really do break through?" he continued. The Sacred Stone seals off the caves to the Dark Land.

"Gaylor's hordes will pour in and turn us into slaves."

"There are extra guards out—"

"They're always doing that. It keeps them on their toes; it keeps *us* on our toes."

"Maybe this time it's real!"

"I'll believe it when I see Lord Gaylor's face myself."

"What do you think he looks like?" (Flay can be such a pain sometimes.)

"How do I know? Black and old, and ugly as a toad. Dripping with Dark Land slime, bristling with warts and moles."

"Good grief!" Flaymonar groaned. He looked so heart-sick that I stopped joking.

"It's just a rumour, Flay; the Stone's for ever more. It has been blessed with spells."

"But he's got counter-spells."

"No one's got spells that good." I gripped his shoulders as I spoke. "We have mages too. Our mages are as good as anything Gaylor has."

"Ours are all old and fat."

"Gaylor's will be too, Flay. Mages are dying out. This is a new age of science and reason—"

"Then why the extra guards who have all got spell-blessed charms?"

"It helps to cheer them up. Gunpowder is the force to turn the Dark hordes back. If they come we'll kill them – we'll blast them into dust. Have you not seen the bombs they tested on the plain?"

"They all blew up in their hands."

"They were the prototypes. They've made them better now." I stepped back gradually, easing myself away. "I really have to go; I have to feed Gravlok."

"With what?"

"The best I've found is four rock-bottom sprouts, and a chicken killed last week."

"That's quite a feast, Cal."

"But he wanted artichokes. I'll have to tart them up with pepper and ginger. Maybe he'll never know."

Fat chance! The Lord Gravlok spotted it instantly.

CHAPTER 3

The next day, limping hard from the beating that Gravlok had given me, I went about my chores. Ours is a large guild and our Hall is full of rooms which all have to be cleaned in strict accordance with the rules. This means that we mutter prayers before we raise a cloth, and repeat them when we're finished. It's all a ritual, as so much of life is here. It helps distract our thoughts from the misery outside. If we had time to think, we would see how meaningless our ancient rituals are …

In the middle of the chores (we were running late that day) the Readying Bell rang.

We dropped our dusters, set aside our mops and stopped muttering our meaningless prayers. We ran through passageways so gloomy that death itself could scarcely be more blind.

We put our robes on and went to raise our lords, who had probably been awake for several hours. They find it hard to sleep, for the echo of the Star still lingers in their brains.

Softly we slip the chains which hold our guild-lords down, frightened that they've gone mad. When madness comes it comes suddenly, and the lords sometimes go berserk. They might strangle their slaves, thinking they're under threat. Guild-guards stand over us, swords poised to run the lords through should they show signs of madness.

But Brodok's as gentle as ever, and sits up with a smile. He rubs his bruised, black wrists and checks them for sores. "Have I gone mad?" he says.

"No, not today, my Lord."

"What a relief!" he sighs.

I dress Brodok in his leaden robe and thick black helm and help him to his chair. It is a wheeled chair which creaks with rot and age, and he wheels it himself through ringing corridors. I walk a pace behind, murmuring prayers to keep him safe.

We make our way to the Ante-room, which is as

far as I can go, for beyond the Ante-room is the Chamber of the Star. No one can enter unless they've spent their lives preparing for that hour. One needs special training in physics and mystic arts. One needs to be prepared physically and mentally. One needs to have the strength to fight a gift from God and not be cowed by it. There is a measure of arrogance in being a Star-Adept; also the stupidity to accept one's certain fate. I tend Brodok with pride, and yet a part of me feels such pity for him.

As I step from the room, the day's chosen Star-Adepts heave one final breath. Every day twenty-four of them are picked to tend the Star, to keep it safe from harm and stop it running wild. They work the rods and chains which liberate the light and help imprison it. They are always silent at this point of the day, knowing that just one door keeps them safe from the Star. I think they worship it and are half in love with it. I also think they are scared of it.

As the servants back away the steel doors of the room slam with a mighty clang. We wait in silence, muttering our private prayers. We know that beyond the doors the Adepts are starting to shake, partly from fear and partly from excitement. Theirs is an eerie wait.

While we stand with heads bowed and hands

tightly clasped in prayer, we hear machinery start up deep within the earth and a rumble as the final door swings wide and the Star-Adepts wheel themselves through.

At this point they are in the 'Chamber,' which no one has ever seen, not even the Star-Adepts themselves, hidden as they are inside their masks. But I've heard that it is large and protected by old runes and sheets of ancient lead.

In the centre of the Chamber a dome covers the Star, and at the given hour chains will winch it aloft. Then the great Star is unleashed, and shafts of light pour out as if Heaven itself had turned to flame.

Through polished shafts and ducts the starlight is channelled up towards Moridor. It passes through lenses and bounces off mirrors. Its power is checked and steered, bent, fractured, measured and teased. Twenty-five major guilds toil to control all this; it is the largest branch of all. We number thousands, those who control the light. We check that it's not too strong, too weak or too dazzling. We check that it feeds the crops, heats water, brings our day, but does not fry us all.

Moridor is a throw-back to a time before the War, when all the world had light and Darkness was contained.

If we should ever fail to keep our Star safe from harm, none of us will remain.

CHAPTER 4

The next day, rumours still persist that the Sacred Stone is cracked.

This stone is a great slab of obsidian flecked with steel, and serves to block a cave which wends beneath our town. The cave is the last route through which Gaylor might come, for all others have been sealed. Our mages have bound the stone with sacrifice and spells and woven mystic charms to keep it safe from harm. They swore no force on earth could ever break it down, but is Gaylor of the earth? Is he not of the Dark now, a creature spurned by God? Are his own black mages more powerful than our own? These rumours haunt us all as they run through the streets, like fire striking kindling.

The guards are doubled, but I have little faith that they will stand and fight if Dark Land armies come. I think they'll turn and flee, for these days sacrifice seems to be in short supply. As I look around me I am filled with shame that the great town of my birth has become so tired and weak. It is so cursed with ritual that all initiative has been squeezed out of it. We have lost something by turning all our power to the protection of our Star; we have turned in on ourselves. It has enslaved us all. No longer is it our tool – we are the tools of the Star. The Star is our new god, master of all our lives. If this thought be blasphemy, then Callibar must blaspheme, for I sense something's wrong. We should have *used* it, not let the Star use us. Sometimes the price we have to pay seems too much. Maybe I'm just upset by the rumours in the town. Maybe they've unsettled me.

For what real alternative could ever be conceived? How could Moridor exist in a world stripped of its light? How could we ever hope to hold Lord Gaylor back without our precious Star?

"Callibar—"

"What?" I said as a trainee woke me, dragging me from slumber.

"Someone is screaming."

"It's the middle of the night. Go back to sleep," I said. "You're just having a dream."

"Alarm bells ring," he added.

"Go back to sleep," I groaned, pushing him from the door. These trainee Adepts are such fear-ridden souls; the slightest little sound sets them off. They have such fear ahead of them that they prepare themselves by having fearful dreams. Part of their training is to instil them with the dread that their lives will disappear if they ever harm the Star. When you are told that at six years old, it must prove quite a weight to take to bed with you.

He was not the first one to have woken me up that way. They wake up screaming out that the Star's light has been dimmed.

I wrapped my head up in my brown blanket, and burrowed back to sleep.

CHAPTER 5

Silence hung in the air when I awoke next day. I knew it was late, for fog filled my brain, and the benefits of sleep had somehow been replaced by that guilt-lethargy which creeps into our bones when we have dreamed too long. No one had called me or shaken me awake, and I knew from the start all was not well that day. The place was too silent, too still and too lonely. Something strange had occurred.

Stumbling from my bed, I pulled on my thin shoes and threadbare clothes. I lurched into the corridor and almost broke my neck when I tripped on a shield dropped by a missing guard. Guards don't leave their posts unless the world should end: theirs is a rigid Guild.

I pulled out a wall-brand, aimed it at the dark and called out Brodok's name, but there was no answer. This place was never that quiet, never that still. I felt as if I were still dreaming.

"My guild-lord Brodok!"

Silence. No rushing feet, no muttering of prayers as the day's chores were performed.

From some distance away came the muted sounds of men talking in low voices.

I walked towards them, through passageways of gloom. I held the brand ahead, but the little light it gave was soon devoured by the shadows engulfing the quiet doorways. Each room was empty, each passageway silent. Each long expanse of gloom seemed deeper than the last. I had seldom been alone or felt so helpless. Where *was* the Star-Guild? Why had everyone disappeared? Why was there so much gloom, instead of channelled light? Why had the guards vanished leaving their swords behind? I kept stepping on discarded weapons.

I entered the Ante-room to find it filled with soldiers streaked with blood.

The massive steel doors had been ripped down and were blackened by fire. The Chamber door itself had been blasted apart. How could I have slept through all that? A night of war had torn our town apart.

"Where's Brodok?" I said. No one answered me. They were too stunned, too busy licking wounds. I found Brodok myself, huddled inside a room where furniture is stored.

"My guild-lord Brodok?"

His eyes glanced up at me, hunted and full of fear. He was sitting on a long couch from which the stuffing protruded. He wore his grey nightshirt, and it was rumpled round his knees. His long white fleshy legs were angled like the arms of some strange catapult.

"Has someone harmed you?"

"No one has harmed me, Cal."

"The Star?"

"The Star has gone – all hope has been destroyed." My lord gazed into my eyes with a look I'd never seen: a look of hopelessness.

"It can't be wiped out—"

"The Star has been removed. Swordsmen came in the night and plundered the town. They have taken the Star."

"That is not possible—"

"The Star has been removed."

As I watched, spittle rolled down Lord Brodok's chin and a strange gleam in his eyes resolved to maddened pain. Suddenly he leapt up.

"Moridor dies now!" he screamed. "Our light has been destroyed and we are lost in the dark!"

I tried to calm him, but he was far beyond my reach.

"Look to yourself, boy! Flee before Gaylor comes! Take to the hills and dig down in the dirt! Dig holes in which to die – vast graves for each of us. This is the end of all!"

Then he rushed off, shrieking, into the gloom, and I shook like a leaf as his madness chilled my soul.

I knew his words were true when the brand died in my hands and total darkness came.

CHAPTER 6

I went into the town and saw the trail of death the Dark Land force had wrought. Through streets of slaughter I traced their every step, seeing each home they had burned, each soldier they had cut down. Our warriors had fought and died with bravery. They had died in anguish, run through with sword and spear or crushed beneath the wheels of carts the Dark force brought. They had fought to save our Star from being hauled away, and died knowing they had failed. Nobleness was no match for Dark Land savagery. In this world the strong survive, and the Dark Land force which came was stronger than our own.

It was just after midnight, so my friend

Flaymonar told me, that the Sacred Stone was smashed and the Dark hordes flooded in, galloping through the streets on horses black as night, led by treacherous guides.

They had stormed the Star Guild while I slept like a babe. (I found out later on that I was not alone in that. Maybe they had cast a spell to trap us in sleep. Maybe spies had drugged our food.)

The doors were blasted open by kegs of gunpowder, which set the sky ablaze and made the city shake. Then they had spurred their great steeds through the gaps the powder breached, and thundered through our halls.

Most guards still standing were cut down where they stood. The fat Adept, Lord Gravlok, was hacked down in an aisle. He was the only lord who ran to save the Star, and I had always mistrusted him!

Then they dragged more blasting kegs through the Ante-room, and blew apart the doors which guard the Star Chamber. They lifted up the Star, still shielded by its dome, and swung it onto a cart made of steel plate, which rumbled like a storm as a dozen jet-black steeds laboured to haul it away. There was great treachery involved in all of this. Moridorians had sold our Star, but as soon as it had been taken they were cut down, killed by the Dark Land warriors, their faithless paymasters.

Then the steel cart rolled away, protected by a

force of Dark Land cavalry which slew all in its path. They rode back to the cave where their journey had begun and vanished with our Star, leaving behind dead and dying soldiers and burning stalls and homes. The light cast by the flames shed a ruddy glow which burned on through the night, but could not bring our dawn.

CHAPTER 7

The shock the Star's loss caused was like nothing we'd known in all our history. We felt numb and empty inside, as if our lives had been ripped apart. The dreaded Dark Land hordes had penetrated our midst and claimed our greatest prize. Our soldiers and prayers had failed us, and all our rituals were simply swept aside. We were lost in the dark, and the only lights which showed were the tiny flames we lit.

On the day after the raid I scaled the city's walls to gaze out on the plain surrounding Moridor. There was nothing but twilight everywhere I looked. No hint of the sun appeared, though it was near midday. Nothing moved in the dust.

What does Gaylor want with it? I wondered. Why destroy? Why wipe out everything which keeps the world from waste? Is this the prize he seeks – an empty, arid plain stretching for ever more? As I brooded, a boy approached. He was holding out his hands, in which he clutched all the wealth that he possessed. He was a somewhat small boy of delicate design, and his blue, sombre eyes were hooded by fear. His skin was deathly pale, and tear-trails scarred the ash which had settled over him.

"Callibar, I'm afraid. Will you say prayers for me?"

I nodded. "Yes, I will."

"This is all my money—"

"You don't bribe for a prayer. Keep all your money hidden and say some prayers yourself. And don't feel so afraid."

His blue eyes glistened with tears. His thin, pale fingers shook. "I can't help it," he said. "Don't you feel scared inside?"

"No, I have faith," I said, almost flinching at my lie. In truth I was afraid, so scared that my heart was like a beating drum inside me. I said, "We have strong warriors who will hunt down the Star and reclaim it. They will bring it back to us, and we'll repair the Sacred Stone."

"Is this the truth?" he said.

I nodded. "Yes, it is." (Lying begets more lies.)

"So we have hope, then?"

"We always have some hope. While the Star still exists, Darkness cannot prevail."

"But if Gaylor kills the Star?"

I stared into his eyes. I could not answer that.

When I descended to the town I found the streets filled with angry citizens. They wanted action; they wanted their Star back. They could not comprehend why our soldiers would not ride out after it. But I could understand: the soldiers had seen death and had been cowed by it. They found many reasons for not pursuing the Star: they were setting up barricades, fault-finding, making plans. The longer they made plans the less time remained to act, such is the way of things.

I shared in the people's anger, but I looked into the soldiers' eyes. They were just lads like me, well-trained but frail inside. I would not go myself, so why send those poor youths out to a near-certain doom? We needed heroes, not trembling boys. We needed men with no reason to survive. We needed men who would die believing that their deaths were worth more than their lives. As I looked around me, I saw no such desperate souls – none with reason enough to die on the Dark Land's poisoned soil. Bravery must give way sometimes, for lost causes are no causes at all.

*　　*　　*

"Callibar—" A fellow novice appeared like a shadow at my side, and pulled me by the sleeve.

"What is it?" I said.

"You must return," he said. "The Adepts are afraid, and are sealing up the Guild. They're raising barricades – they think we will be blamed for not saving the Star."

I said, "That's not our fault—"

"They are stocking up for a siege. Collect all the food you can and return right away. Already quite a crowd has gathered in the square before the Hall's main doors."

I said, "That's crazy. It was not our fault."

"Do you think they care?" he said. "They want to burn us down. The soldiers will not fight and the people scream for blood. It's ours they're looking for."

The novice was not joking; I could see it in his face. He wore the haunted look of one about to die. I must have looked the same, for I was duty bound to try to save the Guild.

"The Hall-guards?" I said.

"The Hall-guards have all fled. We'll take up swords ourselves—"

"I've never held a sword."

"Now is the time to try. We're breaking out the arms. It's time to fight or die."

CHAPTER 8

Halfway across the crowded square which stands before the guild doors, I heard a murmuring. Riders were approaching from the main gate to the east – four men on tall grey steeds, long swords strapped to their sides. They were much like the men I had seen on the plain only four days ago – war-hardened warriors. You could tell it by their eyes: their eyes had looked on death and not been cowed. They had claimed death for their own, and fastened it to their spears. Their eyes were empty.

As the men rode by, silence descended on the crowd and a passageway appeared to let them through. No one stood in their way or dared to challenge them for bringing death into our town.

I joined the silent crowd which followed the four horsemen into the heart of town. I was fairly certain they were of the army I had seen, the one heading north towards the Field of Blood. Something must have drawn them back; maybe they sensed that we were weak and ripe for tasting war. Maybe they were going to destroy us all, unless we offered peace. Maybe this was a team sent to negotiate. Maybe they carried scrolls on which terms were laid down for our surrender. Whatever the motives of the warriors, they seemed quite without fear, and nothing made them look around or miss their stride. They merely trotted on until they reached a spot deemed fit for bargaining.

A hush fell on the town as the tallest of the men cast back his thick grey hood. He was a Drang-mi-laran, pale-skinned and stern of eye – a soldier from the east, well-versed in battle-lore. The Drang-mi-laran tribes had led the last assault in the final days of war. I thought they all had been wiped out, but clearly some remained unless these men were ghosts, from an army of the dead. (Many ghosts stalk the plain, victims of Dark Land spells which rip the souls from men.)

The Drang-mi-laran's cape fluttered as he rose up to gaze about our town. Standing high in the stirrups he looked tall as a god, and I stared down at the ground as his eyes swivelled my way. His gaze flicked past my face like a breath of winter wind, chilling me to the core. We were not brave people then, we guardians of the Star, and we had tried to forget about war in the hope that it would vanish. But war kept coming back like a cancer, which hides but is not gone.

"I see no army here in this city of the Star. I see few warriors." The Drang-mi-laran pulled off his leather gloves and let his right hand rest on the hilt of his black broadsword. The three riders at his back sat as still as statues. Steam rose from their horses into the air.

"Nobody challenged us, or tried to bar the gate. You seem content for strangers to walk your streets. Are you too weak to fight, so brave you bite your tongues?"

Nobody answered him.

After a moment he sat down on his horse, pulled a dagger out, and offered it to one of the crowd. "We have come in peace," he said. "This is a token of our trust. You can run me through with it." When nothing happened, he cried: "My name is Brizek, Prefect of the last brigade of the Drang-mi-laran tribes. We were heading north, but thought to rest a while near the warmth of your fabled Star. Alas, it is gone!" He laughed without humour. "Plucked from your town while all your warriors slept!" (That was not strictly true; a lot of good men had died. But no one corrected him.)

"You let it go!" he said with disbelief. "More than a day has passed by while you wring your hands. You are going to stone your guild rather than raise a force to bring the Star's light back. What madness is this? Have you no will to fight? Are you prepared to watch Lord Gaylor steal your Star? While you weep your Star rolls across the Dark Land soil, farther away with every passing hour." The Drang-mi-laran looked angry, as though he had the right to ride into our town and tell us what was wrong. But, oddly, no one contradicted him; it was as if we saw his point and were ashamed. "Raise an army! Ride out and bring it back! The Star was all you had; how can you watch it leave?"

Our Town-Lord Kreek spoke up. "That's our affair," he snarled. "It is not your business to question what we do. What plans we might engage are there for us to know."

"The light belonged to the world," the Drang-mi-laran said. "You merely guarded it. Perhaps if you had shared it it would not have been taken, but no, you locked it up behind your high stone walls. While others fought in wars you hid your heads in sand, perfecting rituals."

"The Star was *our* Star!"

"The Star plunged to earth. You merely salvaged it."

"And learned how to harness it!" Kreek's face was red with blood; the fury in his soul flared up in angry waves. "Nobody else did! We learned to brave the Star! A thousand mages died learning the secret arts!"

"Arts which remained secret so that none could share the light, or save it when it's lost," interrupted Brizek.

"The Star is not lost – one day we'll bring it back!" Kreek insisted.

"When?" Brizek said softly. "When Gaylor's bled it dry? When there is nothing left but a husk of useless rock? How long will this take?"

Oddly enough, at this point I saw some people nod, for Brizek had made a point which quite a lot of us agreed with. Many could not understand why our own town's great leaders had done nothing so far.

"Gaylor will drain it until Darkness rules the world, and you'll still be sitting here with your heads in the sand."

"Yes, Kreek!" somebody cried from the back of the sombre crowd. "When will we bring the Star back? Where is our army? Why don't we ride to war?"

"Because we made a vow that we would forsake war!" Kreek put a weary hand to his face. "It's written in the scrolls which govern how we live. We have an army merely for self-defence —"

"Much good they did us!" the same voice shouted back. "What will they defend next – the ruins of our town after Gaylor's hordes ride through? We want some *action*!"

"We are not equipped to fight. We can't tread Gaylor's land if we are not prepared."

"So we're just going to die?" somebody else shouted. "Some great leader you are, Kreek!"

"Listen, it's not *my* fault—"

Brizek held up his hand. "That's why we're here," he said. "We've come to make a deal. We'll try to save your Star."

"What with? An army made up of one brigade?"

"We travel light and fast, and can overtake the Star. With luck we'll bring it back long before Lord Gaylor can get his hands on it."

"Ha!" Kreek looked scornful. "You know the Dark Land, then? You know where Gaylor lurks? You know the Death Palace?"

"We'll learn much more than you who sit here wringing your hands," Brizek said quietly. "This is the offer, Kreek: we'll go and find your Star, and in return you'll give a piece of it to us. You'll show us how it works, how to control its light – and then we'll ride away."

"Where to?"

"Our homeland, where we must bury our dead; for the Drang-mi-lars are doomed and we are all that remains. We want to die in peace, with light filling our eyes: that's why we make this offer. While you have been 'learning' and playing with your Star, most of the world has died, withered up like a plague. The Drang-mi-lars at least will leave this earth like men, not vermin."

The riders wheeled around and their horses reared and stamped. "We'll wait up in the hills while you work out your reply," said Brizek. "When you've decided, send that boy," he pointed at me. "The boy's seen us before."

So the riders had recognized me when they thundered through the plain, though I had crouched down low and burrowed in the dirt! How could they see so well that they knew my face? Truly, they were special.

CHAPTER 9

While the elders of our town met in closed conference, I sought my friend Flaymonar. "What do you think, then?" I asked him.

"We've got nothing to lose," he said. "No one from Moridor will go to the Dark Land. You saw what Kreek was like – he was quaking in his boots. The others are all the same." He picked a pebble up and threw it against a wall. "Our town is built on sand, and our strength is the same. It trickles through our hands when we need steel and rock to fortify our minds. We need some *heroes*."

I nodded. "We're short of them."

"We need men who are not afraid to take on Lord Gaylor. I bet they'll send you, too."

"What for?"

"Somebody said they want a Star-Adept."

I gave a short laugh. "They'll hardly send *me* down. I'm not a Star-Adept, nor will I ever be."

Flay shrugged as he aimed for a lantern on a wall, and threw another stone. "You're in the guild, Cal; who else are they going to send? At least you're a Senior; all the rest are novices."

"They'll send a Star-Adept!"

"Half of your lords have fled and the others are insane. Can you see Lord Brodok travelling underground?"

"Then they'll promote a mage."

Flay grunted. "Don't be daft! A mage go underground, down into Gaylor's realm? Dream on, sweet Callibar!"

He kept on hurling pebbles against the crumbling wall and I watched each one land in a tiny puff of dust. I thought he must be mad to think they'd send me down, but I felt sick inside.

"No, I can't ride a horse," I said to the Beast-master who was equipping me for my trip. "I rode a donkey once for a hundred yards."

"That's good enough," he snarled, heaving me on to an ass. It was an old grey beast which moved at slightly less than a sick snail's crawling pace. "This is an old beast, but she's steady as a rock. Another ass might spook if I sent it on to the plain."

"What about me?" I said. "I might get spooked myself."

"That isn't my problem." He tossed a stick to me and said, "Prod her with that, but don't hit her too hard or she's liable to throw you off. She's got a nice nature as long as all you do is what she wants to do."

He flexed his muscles as I looked round nervously. This was not quite the way I thought it was going to be. I had waited all my life to be given the chance to shine, and here I was, clinging to an old grey ass.

I said, "This is a momentous day in the history of Moridor, and it seems the whole thing rests on the good nature of an ass."

The tattooed Beast-master gave a shrug. "This world is often strange. Do you want to take a horse?"

"No thank you," I said. "I'd better stick to the ass."

The man gave a sneering grin, and said, "Get going then!" I wondered if he knew how much depended on me. I wondered if he cared.

"Where do I go now?" I said.

"Don't ask me," he muttered. "I merely tend the beasts." He steered me through the door.

"We're not well organized."

"This town has never been organized, except for rituals." Then he took pity on me. "The best of luck!" he said.

I said, "Do you think we'll win?"

"Win what?"

"Win back the Star?"

"What's happened to the Star?"

That man had spent too long shovelling horse manure.

I rode back into town to find the populace crammed into the market square. All of our dignitaries were standing in their robes on a hastily-erected stage which towered above the throng. A fanfare sounded out as my grey ass appeared, and a ragged cheer went up. People were applauding, though it was mostly for the ass, for she was the oldest ass living in Moridor. "Ah, bless her!" they cried, hardly looking at me as I prodded her on.

My turn was to come, though, when I reined in at the foot of the short flight of steps which led up to the stage, and the Priestess Mandridar came down and clutched my hand while Lord Kreek made a speech. She was the Priestess of Sacrifice, which rather worried me, so that I could not hear the words Lord Kreek was spouting. All I could think was, 'Who is it? Who is the sacrifice?' And my thoughts kept coming back to me.

I didn't want to go out there if I was going to die. Why should I have to die?

Mandridar sensed my fear. "Be noble," she said.

"I'm not brave, Mandridar."

"You're brave enough," she said. "You're braver than Lord Kreek. It's not for you they fear, it is for their own souls. They're weak, but you are strong."

That was my pep talk, and as I stared into her eyes I could see that she was trying hard to give me strength. Her eyes were red with the bloodshed she had seen; with those years of sacrifice.

"What will they do with me?"

"Nothing," Mandridar said. "You merely take the scroll which Lord Kreek will pass down. Then we'll put spells on you to guide you on your way, and pray for your return."

That was the kind of thing that worried me, the 'praying for my return'. Did Mandridar know something she wasn't telling me? Or was it just my fear making me paranoid?

"Why can't a warrior go?"

"They asked for you, Cal," she said, squeezing my hand. Few get to feel the touch of the Priestess of Sacrifice.

"I feel sick," I said.

"Are you a hero?"

"No, I'm just Cal."

"Then that's your greatest strength," she said. "Just be yourself. You have nothing to prove except that you have the strength to ride out on the plain."

While we were talking, Lord Kreek was winding up, saying some things about nobility. It made me feel quite proud until I realized that he was talking about himself.

CHAPTER 10

The whole town watched me leave, and Mandridar herself escorted me to the gates. I was clutching a thin scroll on which our town's reply was written out in blood, as a sign of its importance. It was tied with a length of silk held in place by the Town-Guild's seal, and weighed nothing at all. So delicate was it that I feared it might blow away, and I tucked it into my shirt, where it nestled on my breast. So tiny – so much power. So much significance written with a dead crow's blood.

I headed through the gloom which lay around the town like a dull blanket. Only faint shadows were discernible through that gloom and beyond there was nothing at all. An empty-sounding wind whispered across a land formed out of soil and bone. So many warriors had died on the plain that their dust now rose up in clouds like muddied chalk. I was breathing the bones of men slaughtered in long-gone wars. The ass crushed ancient skulls beneath her feet.

Three hours of slow riding brought me to the base of the long, thin ridge on which the warriors were camped. I could see their small fire, a weak and frail affair. I could hear their snorting steeds and the creak of old leather. I could hear men whispering as if they marked each step of the wavering course I took. The ass was tiring, and reluctant to approach the knot of black horses which stood in her way. I had to turn her loose and continue on my own, scrambling up the last few feet.

On the ridge I faced a ring of faces pale as ghosts, with eyes keen as steel. They watched me as I stumbled on the bones which littered the cold ground, but offered no help. I thought it was a test to see how I performed, and that I did not do well. I lost all dignity as I crashed down in a heap. Some of the warriors laughed, and one threw rocks my way. I said, "I've brought a scroll." I was growing quite annoyed at the way they treated me.

"Then bring it closer," a voice said.

I threw it on the ground. "Fetch it yourself," I said. I had gone as far as I chose; this was my chance to show how tough I was. But none of them took it; they merely stared at me, and in the end I had to pick it up and hold it out to them.

One said, "Read it aloud."

"It's too dark," I replied, but he tossed a brand to me. There was nothing I could do but rip away the seal and unfasten the scroll. With the brand clutched between my knees I bent over the page and read: *"We take your terms."*

"Is that it?" queried Brizek.

"That's all it says," I said. "Except for Lord Kreek's name, and one that I can't read."

"They're a tight-lipped bunch of men."

I said, "They feel ashamed to have to call on you for help."

CHAPTER 11

After some quiet debate the warriors broke camp and rounded up their steeds. I stood amongst them, as lost as any unarmed youth in a crowd of men with swords hanging from their belts. Some time elapsed before I realized that half of them were women. At last I recognized that what Brizek had said – *"we are all that remains"* – was the literal truth. These were the very last of the mighty Drang-mi-lars; this group was all they had. An entire nation had been whittled down to some two hundred souls, who were now climbing onto their jet-black steeds. I realized just how long my town of Moridor had closed its eyes to the world.

"Are you surprised, boy, that there are so few of us?" It was Brizek who spoke.

"I thought there were more," I said. "I thought out on the plain —"

"The whole great plain is dead." Brizek wheeled away from me as someone retrieved the ass, and I climbed on to its back and followed in his wake. What a sad band we made, but how noble they were! I liked those Drang-mi-lars.

"Hey, boy!"

I glanced around as a girl reined in her steed beside my labouring beast. She was a somewhat slight girl, though she looked stronger than I, and she had the scars of war emblazoned on her cheeks. Her long auburn hair was bundled up inside her battered helm and her clothes were dusty and tattered, streaked with mud. The breastplate that she wore was pitted with small holes and rust showed on the links of mail which covered her arms. Only her sword was clean.

"Your name is Callibar?"

"That's right."

"What does it mean?"

"It means 'Nothing at all'. An ancient family name." I was trying to make a joke, but it did not make her laugh, she was too grave for that. She merely watched me as though I was a freak of nature.

"Why do they call you that?"

"Because I have no rank and will not rise to one."

The girl nodded as though this meant something, but something meant for her rather than for myself. "So it is true that your Moridor has now become such a rigid place that your destiny is ordained?"

"What?" I frowned at her.

"You are from a town of rules. Rituals guide your every move, and you act much as its slaves."

"It isn't quite like that."

"How is it then?" she asked.

I wished she had not asked me that. I felt defensive as I tried to explain our rules, show how each tiny part goes to make up the whole. I said, "We're little cogs inside a great machine."

"Or a machine of cogs."

"Look, girl, what is this?"

"My name is Julivette. It means 'Star of the East', which is nicer than your name."

"So what?" (I'd changed my mind. I now thought these Drang-mi-lars were quite an arrogant lot.) It did not help me that I was on an ass while she was on a horse which towered over me. I wanted a horse myself, except they looked so fierce that they rather startled me. Those beasts were war-beasts which had survived the last affray. They had seen the flashing swords of

Gaylor's raving hordes. The most that I had ever seen was a fight in the market square between two stall-holders.

"Don't get so touchy," she said.

"I merely think you're wrong."

"You don't like 'Julivette'?"

"That isn't what I mean."

"What do you mean?" she asked.

"Stop picking on my town."

"As you wish," she replied.

Then she spurred her horse away, leaving me to choke on clouds of dust, but I gamely plodded on in the trail the war-beasts carved. I felt as small as a shrimp swimming among the sharks off our world's far-distant shores.

CHAPTER 12

When we reached Moridor I had the strange feeling that we were riding into Hell. An eerie silence hung across the town, as if all the people were dead and only ghosts remained – ghosts which slipped through the tracts of shade which encircled burning brands and smouldering braziers. Smoke drifted skyward, then settled back to earth. Dogs slunk in moody packs, avoiding human eyes. A smell of corruption rose from great piles of filth which rotted in the streets. In the absence of the Star's light my town was winding down and grinding to a halt as its people wrestled with despair. Tools slipped from disillusioned hands as thoughts turned from the present to a future without hope.

I soon found myself overlooked in the stir the horse-warriors caused as they advanced into the town. Curious townsfolk surrounded them as they clattered through the streets, the thunder of their horses' hooves booming out ahead and their long cloaks, darker than smoke, spreading like a midnight cloud across the seething throng. From every window people gazed down. From every dim doorway eyes glimmered like dark pearls. The band of warriors was the most dramatic thing Moridor had seen for a while.

As I trailed behind I realized that this was no place for a youth on an old grey ass, and I turned away. I sought the Beast-master to return the ass to him, but he had joined the throng, so I brushed down the ass myself, and locked her in a stall where dry straw lined the floor. Then I sat down to consider all I'd seen, and what it meant to me.

It meant excitement and danger and it might even mean war. I was aware that we weren't alone in the fight against the Dark Land, and despite his best attempts some were still brave enough to challenge Gaylor's will. My own town was weak and scared, and I was ashamed of it for not showing better grace. I wished we had fought ourselves instead of buying help from passing mercenaries. I had actually counted them as we rode towards the gates, and there were two hundred heads, not one more, not one less. My town was thousands strong, yet we could not raise a force to chase the Star ourselves.

So what did that make us, cowards or wise men? Do fools go out to fight or do they stay behind?

I must have fallen asleep, for some time after that someone awakened me. I looked up blearily to see the tall Brizek bending down over me, shaking me by the arm. He said, "I have bad news."

"What's up?"

"You have to come to act as Star-Adept."

"*What?*"

"Your town's elders have agreed to send someone with knowledge of the Star, to help us bring it back. But no one volunteered – in fact they all ran off. You are the only one left."

I said, "But that's impossible!" as I struggled to sit up, brushing straw from my hair and flicking ticks from my clothes. "They can't go running off! What about Lord Brodok?"

"No one knows where he is."

"I have no knowledge, though —"

"Don't you see, Cal?" he said. "They are all afraid to go, and so they offer you. They think our quest is doomed, but they make use of you as some kind of compromise." He sat down beside me with a creak of old leather, and swung his sword aside. "This town is not brave. In fact, if I were you I'd be ashamed of it."

"I *am* ashamed!" I said, clambering to my feet. "They can't send me down there; I know nothing at all!"

"But you know more than us," he said. "Without your help, the Star could destroy us all. We've never seen it – we don't know what to do."

"Neither do I," I said. "*I've* never seen the Star!"

"Would you send us alone?"

"Don't ask me things like that," I said, half-choked with fear. "They can't send *me* down – I'd just be in the way."

"Are you afraid to go?"

"Of course I am!" I said.

"Then we must go alone," said Brizek, gazing down on me with deep and sombre eyes.

CHAPTER 13

For two days I wrestled with my guilt while I watched the Drang-mi-lars make their preparations for the campaign. Somewhere inside me I knew that I would have to go, for the shame my refusal caused me would ultimately outweigh my fear; but I hung on desperately, hoping that someone else would rise to take my place. No one did, though, for they were all as scared as me, and in a town of frightened souls one is as much good as the next. People offered me some advice, saying, "You'll be fine," but that was as far as it went. No one actually came up to me saying, "I'll ride along. Two swords are better than one if it should come to a fight." I did not know which was worse: my shame for Moridor, or my shame at my own fear.

While all this wrestling was going on inside my head, the warriors made themselves ready and said their final prayers to whichever gods they served. They loaded up a cart with fodder for their steeds and polished up their swords. They had sketched out a very rough map with the aid of our scouts and scribes, but from what I saw of it, it was not going to help much. All it showed was that past the Sacred Stone and the extensive caves beyond lay a land of mystery. We had never been down there, and none had come to us, and what knowledge we had gleaned was guesswork as much as fact. We knew only that there Darkness ruled.

This desperate, heroic quest was cursed when it began, setting off in blindness to a land never yet seen. Yet still I went with them.

"I thought you would not come," said Brizek as I strove to calm my wayward horse. I had discovered that I had a natural riding ability, but only on an ass. A horse is something else, but I thought that if I could manage to survive at least as far as the cave entrance, I would have proved something.

Mustering some irony, I said, "I was growing bored here, living a peaceful life."

"I'm not surprised," he said.

"But I don't want to die."

"Neither do I," he said. "So we have much in common, although we have barely met."

Unlike me and my horse.

The Sacred Stone had cracked into a thousand shards, and each one had been scarred by fire. This seemed so impossible that I stared at it with an empty heart. No one in Moridor could have concocted such a spell. No one in Moridor could have caused that stone to smash like a glass dropped on a floor.

For twelve millennia the Sacred Stone had kept us safe from the Dark hordes underground, over which Gaylor now ruled. It had sealed the Dark Land caves and had been our security and strength and the most sacred of our shrines. To see it in fragments was like watching a god come tumbling down to earth and die at one's feet. Gods are not supposed to die, and Sacred Stones can't break, but this one was destroyed.

Such powerful evidence of a force greater than ours made our quest appear doomed before we had even made a start, and as I turned to watch the crowd which had gathered to see us off I saw my fear reflected in its eyes. The people had no hope for us and were merely clutching at straws, sending brave fools out on errands fit for fools.

Such a wave of apathy proved a chilling test of faith, but I thought that if I was doomed to die then at least I would see something other than the streets of Moridor first. Maybe I would die as soon as I stepped into the cave. Maybe I would one day return as a hero, dressed in gold. Maybe I would never know.

Moving in a hushed convoy we descended into the cave from which the Dark Force had come. It was a cold and vast place in which our torchlight soon died, swallowed up by a gloom spawned at the birth of time – a place so steeped in murk that even our Star's bright light could not have conquered it. The squealing cartwheels and clatter of hooves faded like splashing stones dropped into a silent tide and our voices disappeared as if a huge dark god had snatched them from the air. Clutching my thin cloak tightly around me, I huddled like a child threatened by that great black ghost which lurks beneath the stairs. The hand of Gloom itself fastened around my throat with a grip which choked my breath.

"I'm Finglor," said a female voice, speaking out of a darkness so intense that I could not see her face. "I am Julivette's mother and leader of this band."

I said, "I'm Callibar, the smallest voice of all."

"Not small at all," she said. "You have the strength within to handle the great bright Star. You have the secret power."

"I don't, though," I said. "I don't know much at all."

"But you are wise enough to know that you should come with us."

"Wisdom?" I muttered. "Is that what this quest is all about?"

She laughed. "Or bravery. Or plain stupidity."

Then she steered her horse away and rode off, still laughing, while I stared at a gloom which was so dense it hurt. I thought, *These Drang-mi-lars, are they laughing at me? Or don't they really care?*

Strung out like necklace beads, and with silence all around, we proceeded through the gloom. Our only comfort lay in the grim belief that every cave had an end and we must be patient. Gaylor could not succeed by merely hiding out beyond a midnight veil.

Like dulled moths we trudged on, following the guttering brands of two distant out-riders. They were like faint jewels dancing across a screen of darkness so complete that it seemed like a solid wall.

For two dull, silent days we advanced through the sombre gloom of the enormous cave system. We heard no voices and saw no sign of life other than the occasional marks left by the Darklanders' cart, and the odd charm which they had left to cover their trail with webs of secrecy. They had dropped twisted mage-thongs, designed to interfere with our perception of their trail and the route their convoy had taken. They hoped to send us round in circles, endlessly chasing our own tracks.

I have to say, though, that they did not try too hard to cover up their tracks, for they obviously thought that we would not follow. They probably believed that the threat of Gaylor's land itself would be a sufficient barrier. This led me to two conclusions: firstly, that they knew Moridor well, better than I did myself, for I was still shocked by our disgrace. Secondly, the Drang-mi-lars' presence might not be known to them and this would give us a slight edge. But perhaps they did not care whether our band came or not. Perhaps they were secure in a knowledge of their own strength and our weaknesses. For underneath it all, and despite our bravery, we were only two hundred strong in a land of vast design. How could we hope to win when the mighty Star itself could not blind its Dark foes?

After those first two numbing days we sensed that the cavern's distant walls were tapering ominously, closing into something like a shaft that miners might have left when their vein of gold ran dry. The sounds we made – the grinding of wheels, the drumbeat of hooves – no longer echoed but pounded at us. The claustrophobic gloom, chokingly dense before, gained a new intensity. The change surprised us, for our minds were so numb that we might have plodded on like zombies forever. Any change brought relief and, as yet, we could sense no direct threat to us. Even the two out-riders, who had turned and were heading back, cantered without alarm, their thin brands trailing sparks. We gathered in a group, more curious than scared, to await their report.

"A chasm lies ahead like a great maw in the earth. There is no way around it."

"What of the Darklanders?" asked Finglor.

"A drawbridge straddles the gorge, but not surprisingly it has been winched aloft. Short of an Act of God we can find no way across, save for that single path. We cannot reach it, and I doubt that the Dark Land force will drop the bridge into place so that our party can pursue them. It may be that this is as far as we can go." The out-rider gave a shrug.

"Did you plumb the pit's depth?" Finglor asked.

"We threw down some heavy rocks, but if they ever reached the base we never heard a sound. And there is no way that we could edge around, for the chasm's sides commence their long descent at the foot of the cavern's walls."

"Could we climb down it?"

The out-rider shrugged again. "With wings we

might survive, but we might never reach the floor. This trap smacks of mages' work; such a precise and perfect obstacle could scarcely be natural." The man looked frustrated, and tossed his brand aside as its last thin flame gave up the ghost and died. He said, "I fear that we may have to return, for I could see no way across and doubt that there is one."

Despite the man's misgivings, our band was nothing if not desperate, and so we carried on right to the chasm's lip. However, as we peered out over the edge the out-rider's fears and doubts seemed to be not unwise.

Time passed, with me alone wondering what would befall and the rest debating. It was fairly obvious that there was no way to reach the bridge, and the plan was to descend into the gorge. It was hoped that our store of ropes, when knotted end to end, would prove of sufficient length. I had considerable doubts about this though I kept them to myself, for I expected to be excused owing to my lack of physical skill. However, the upshot of the long debate was that my relative lack of weight proved the deciding factor. It seemed to the warriors a lot more sensible to send the lightest down, bearing in mind that the descent would take quite some time. The chasm wall on this side of the gorge was so sheer that climbing was ruled out, and I would have to be lowered by rope. It would then be up to me to scale the rough wall opposite and let the drawbridge down so that the warriors could cross. They had more faith than me if they thought I could do that. There was more chance that pigs might fly!

My instinctive reluctance was tempered by the fact that the only real alternative was the abandonment of our quest, and the thought that I alone would be the one to bear the blame for our failure back home in Moridor.

"I'm shaking," I said.

Julivette said, "Then I'll go, too. I will act as his bodyguard in case this is a trap."

Her brave words put me to shame at the precise moment at which I'd planned to settle for shame.

After an hour of slow descent a brand went tumbling past, spreading light through the gloom. From our leather harnesses we watched it spiral down, a tiny beam of hope in the void. But somewhere far below it died without a sound, lost in the great darkness. My gaze turned upwards, towards the distant cave where two teams of men lowered us grimly hand over hand. They were so far away that it seemed getting back again would be impossible. We were like baskets swinging from tiny threads; two helpless lumps of flesh for the darkness to embrace. When the brand's light disappeared the silence which followed was a ferocious thing.

"I've never cared for heights," I said.

"Neither have I," Julivette murmured.

"Do you think it makes a difference, not being able to see the floor?"

"I don't find that it helps," she said. "In fact, it makes it worse."

"So why did you offer to come?"

"Because I have to be as strong as my mother. She is a great warrior who leads our people well, and it is up to me to prove that it runs through our line."

"So you didn't do it for me?"

"I like you, Cal," she said, "but I would not die for you. It is only for my mother that I am hanging by this thread."

"Thanks very much," I said.

"Don't mention it," she replied.

My gaze probed far below, but for all that I could see I might as well have been blind.

After two more long hours we seemed little closer to the bottom of the gorge. Maybe the air was different here – I could not really tell. Maybe I felt a breath of wind not felt before. Maybe I heard the sound of water rushing by, but I could not be sure. My every sense was reeling from the assault of the endless gloom, and the occasional brand which hurtled by served only to confuse me more. It was as if I had been offered a glimpse of the Sun and stars themselves, as they were formed from Chaos's stew. I felt like shouting, though I had nothing to say. I felt that life was nothing but dreams, and I must be deep in sleep. My companion Julivette was as silent as any passing thought.

After another hour the sound of water below came clearly to my ears. We were descending steadily towards a rushing tide, and the thought came to me that we could be about to drown. How would the others know, up there on that high ledge which formed the chasm's rim? They would just keep on lowering, letting the long ropes out. They might eventually notice that both ropes had gone slack, but by then where would we be? Gasping and choking for air, with water fast filling our lungs?

"Julivette —" I whispered.

"I hear," she murmured.

"We ought to shed our packs in readiness to dive."

"Dive into what?" she said. "I have never swum before. The eastern plains are dry."

I said, "I'll help you – you can clutch on to me for support."

"A weedy youth like you? I'm more likely to drown."

I said, "Trapped in these harnesses we may very well both drown," and she grunted at me.

But I had made a good point, for the river down below was gnawing at the walls and snarling like a beast. After some quick debate we took out our knives and hacked at the long ropes.

We plunged for thirty feet before crashing into a flow so cold it numbed our bones. Our breath snorted out of us as the shock clutched at our lungs, and angry, hissing foam filled our ears and eyes. I clawed myself up, heaving in gasps of air, and reached out for Julivette. She punched me in the eye. I tried to keep her calm as she snatched at me from behind, grappling with her arms and legs, but I could scarcely prevent myself from drowning. I kept on screaming but she continued to clutch at me, trying to climb onto my back. Finally I grabbed her hair and thrust away from her, then began to tow her like a raft. Several times I almost lost my grip. Numbness caused by the cold, plus the weight of Julivette, almost proved too much for me.

The river carried us through a long, narrow race, a shaft gnawed through the rock. I could only sense this through the pressure on my ears, and the intensity of sound that the tunnel's narrowness caused, but I felt that if I were to raise my hand I

70

might lose my knuckles. Inches above me was a vault of jagged rock, and I did not need to see to know that it was there. My greatest fear was that there might be an outcrop of rock in my path, but this did not materialize. For I had enough problems controlling Julivette, who was still trying to pulverize me. Whether this was caused by fear of death or rage at my technique I could not quite decide, but she did not appreciate being towed along by her hair and swore to take revenge at the first chance she got. I didn't think I'd like that much.

For all its rage and spite the river finally poured through a fracture in the rock. Two hours of battering had left us almost senseless, and we lay and groaned on a narrow shore of ash, surrounded by the chewed remains of rats. The only sign of life was the vultures overhead. We were in a wasteland somewhere within the earth – surely Lord Gaylor's realm, for who but he would live here? Who would live in this place where the only sound to be heard was the scream of silence?

As we slowly regained our breath we began to look around. A grey sky brooded above our heads, but it was not a normal sky – it was a vault of rock, and the light which filled the air came from small phosphor chips embedded in it. It was not like daylight, more like the sick, cold gleam of a poisonous twilight.

But at least we could now see, and would not have to stumble blindly. We could see rolling plains and high mountains. We could see distant towns, and clouds of thick black smoke rising from far-off towers.

Much closer to us was the towering mountain range through whose feet ran the tide which brought us to that spot. The route to Moridor had to be in that range, but probably some way east. It was difficult to estimate how far we had been carried, but it was no doubt several miles. It would be some considerable time before we found the cave and our waiting comrades.

There had to be a pathway of some kind leading to the cave, for the Dark Land raiding force could not have walked on air. When we had recovered enough we set off on a search to find where the path lay.

CHAPTER 14

It took more than a day to find the cave entrance. A wide track approached it, scarred by the weight of hooves. On it lay a twisted mage-thong. The dry grey rock bore a curse written in blood, threatening us with death, but as we skirted around it we covered it with dust. We peered into the cave, hoping that the Dark Land force had not left any guards.

Slowly we crept forward, the light behind fading like dying embers. We found the drawbridge, which was a huge affair fashioned of oak and steel, well-blessed with ancient runes. It took us quite some time to hack away the locks of the restraining bar.

When we had finally released it we let the drawbridge down, and it fell with a crash which made the mountain shake. Great clouds of coal-black dust swirled up to choke our eyes and thunder roared in our ears.

But no one stood there waiting to walk across. No Drang-mi-laran steeds snorted and champed their bits. We could only stand and stare at the empty, silent gloom, and wonder where they'd gone.

"Over there," said Julivette, as we stood on a high stone ledge, gazing across the land. "The nearest landmark is the tower within that town."

"A place which doubtless brims with the servants of Gaylor." I frowned as I peered through the gloom towards the distant sprawl. "They are probably waiting for us to wander down, and getting out their pans ready to boil up our bones."

She said, "This pessimism, is that a trait of Moridor?"

"No, I learned it myself."

My lack of graciousness could perhaps be in part explained by the depressing weight of the cold, unwholesome air. It crawled beneath my skin and niggled at my bones like a corrosive force. The utter loneliness of the place distressed me too. I knew why it was deserted, for who would care to walk abroad when that spectral, bloodied light shone down on every step? It was as if the very air bled and we were forced to inhale its stench with each reluctant breath. This land was Gaylor's tomb: a monument to gloom and his half-crazed desires. But what kind of empire did Lord Gaylor choose to rule if Darkness was the goal he set himself? How could he crave a world deprived of light and shade and stripped of every joy?

"Since nothing moves on the plain, and the town attracts the eye, that is where we must look," said Julivette.

I said, "I must say that you shame me with your hopeful approach, but maybe they've gone back to Moridor."

"Finglor would not leave me. Would your mother leave you?"

"She did," I murmured. "I am an orphan."

"Dying is different," Julivette said softly, shading her eyes as if to hide that sky. "My mother's still alive, so they might be here since they're not in the cave."

"I don't quite follow that," I said. "They *could* be dead. Your logic defeats me on finer points like this. They could have been called back or been forced to turn back—"

"Not Finglor," Julivette replied. "My people would continue to look for me while there was the slightest hope, and hope is what we must have while we try to find them."

As we gazed down at the town we both sensed that they weren't down there, but there was nowhere else to look.

For several weary hours we trudged across the plain towards the Dark Land town. Absolute silence hung in the air, and the only signs of life were the vultures wheeling overhead. We seemed like the last two souls left in the universe as we plodded through the dust. Nobody challenged us, even as we reached the dusty road which came in from the east and wound towards the gates. No sentries stood on guard or peered down from the walls which stood silent as ghosts. If we were pillagers we could have robbed at will; if we had come to trade we would have travelled in vain. Not one whisper of wind broke through the corrupting gloom which sprawled across the town.

As we ventured through its streets we felt like two watchmen assigned to patrol a tomb. There were no lanterns in the brackets on the walls. No charcoal throbbed with heat in the braziers of the squares. No children played with balls, no dogs growled, no one called. No one appeared at all. This was nothing but an empty ghost town which must once have thrived, judging by the trappings of its halls. We learned its name from a sign tacked to a wall. The town was *Bakkmalar*.

"There's no one here," I said, as we stood in the town's main square, weary and streaked with dust. "This is a place which even ghosts avoid. The people are all dead, or else they've moved away."

"There were some horses in the stalls."

"They must have been left behind."

"Who feeds and waters them?"

I was too tired to answer that, and too numb to care. All I wanted to do was find somewhere to rest. I said, "Let's find a bed."

She said, "Let's find *two* beds."

"Suits me," I muttered back.

I crawled between the sheets of a bed so old it creaked like the branches of a tree. It was in the bedroom of the best building in town – a place which must have housed a lord in days gone by, a place which was now home to spiders as big as rats and rats as big as dogs. I'd had to fight them for the right to claim the room, slashing out with my sword until they withdrew and settled in other dark rooms along the corridor. Then I barricaded the door with a chest and a throne-like chair, and reassured myself that there were no holes through which the beasts might pass, before settling down on the bed and drawing the thick curtains which hid me from the world. I wedged a tallow candle into the bed's headboard, and felt as rich as I had felt in my whole life. Never before had I known such luxury as a four-poster bed.

Of course there's a price to pay for stealing someone's bed, even if they're not around. The thought that they might come back again makes it hard to sleep, and of course one doesn't know what went on in that bed in the past. It might be home to ghosts; it might have known death; the dust could be disease. So I slept fitfully despite my weary mind, and woke several times as my nightmares ran amok. I thought I could hear sounds; I thought I could feel things brushing across my face.

"Julivette —"

"What?"

"What happened to your face?"

"A spider bit it," she said. "It injected a poison which is eating through my flesh, dissolving all the bones, making the skin peel away. Look —"

"I don't want to look," I said. "Don't make me look."

She said, "You have to look."

Julivette made me sit watching her while she slowly fell apart, and lumps of poisoned skin dropped from her melting flesh, and the screams which I could hear came not from her but from my own shocked heart.

It was absolute agony that I felt as she dissolved; an embrace of all the pain that she refused to feel herself. Only when the terrible pain increased to a level that I could not stand did I find myself jerked awake ...

"Hell's teeth!" I bellowed as a long-legged hairy beast scuttled across the bed. A jet-black spider, bigger than a cat, was heading for my face on legs like angled stilts. It was coming like a blur, silent and grim as death, streaking over the sheets. I had no chance to evade it for it came so fast and my mind was still caught up in the dream I'd just endured. Then it sprang, and crashed down on my cheek!

Like the fingers of a hand its legs enfolded me in an obscene embrace. I was stiff with terror as the thin claws gripped my face and the long fangs flexed and probed, then lay down flat again. Soft, sensory palps roamed over the sweat which drenched my cheeks and trickled past my lips.

Then with a dry-leaf quivering the spider braced its legs, as if prepared to wait for me to provoke a strike. It wanted me to move, it wanted me to try to flick it from my face.

"Are you okay in there?"

I dared not make a sound to warn Julivette of my plight. I was still rigid beneath the spider's weight, scared to make a move in case its tense fangs struck. I could not reach the knife which lay beneath the sheets, a hand's-breadth from my grip.

I wanted to kill it but I knew that it would win, for I sensed this was a game which the spider had long planned. The beast had done this before, and dark malevolence burned in its eyes.

"Why is the door locked?" I heard her give a shove and my clumsy barricade let out a warning creak. It wasn't built to last – it was protection from rats, not Julivette's whole weight.

"There's something blocking it."

She shoved the door again. I felt the spider tense as the chest crashed to the floor. I thought, *If she comes in and whips these curtains back the spider will react ...*

Very gingerly I reached towards my knife, not daring to breathe out in case I made the spider strike. My fingers grabbed the hilt and, an inch at a time, I slid the blade up my chest.

"There's a big box here!" Julivette gave a final shove and the barricade collapsed as I jerked and thrust the knife. But even as I moved the spider's razored fangs plunged down into my cheek.

At once a searing pain went racing through my cheeks, burning from ear to ear. I could feel my flesh dissolving as the venom spread like oil, creeping through every inch of the muscles of my face. With a grotesque delight the spider bit again, flooding my face with pain. Its fangs plunged into me as I arched on the bed, raising one desperate hand to pluck the creature off. But as I grabbed its back and squeezed it like a rag, darkness spread over me …

My oblivion was disturbed by bouts of searing pain which glowed like poppyfields. Great clouds of thunder trundled across a sky where spectres rode on steeds called forth from Hell-like dreams. Dead men walked on the land with flails, beating the few mortals who survived. Women and children were herded into lakes. Soldiers fell on their swords. Towns collapsed beneath the wheels of growling battle carts which slowly crushed the earth. This desperate nightmare was as much a vision of the past, when Gaylor's maddened hordes threatened to rule the world, as a portent of the future – a forewarning of a time when Gaylor would rise again.

As the visions died away a new nightmare appeared in the shape of a spectre. A sallow, corpse-like face was looming close to mine; a deep-eyed, haggard crone whose skin hung down in folds, and whose hand was so thin it was but bone, painted to look like flesh. When I writhed away from her she forced me to return. When I cried in fear and shock she smiled a toothless smile. When I winced she plunged her hand far down into my pain, and tore the roots from it. And throughout all this she murmured exotic chants and prayers, while swinging golden lamps mere inches from my face. The lamps poured out a smoke which writhed about my eyes, heady and thick with scent.

"Callibar!" sighed the crone. "Fight to shake off your dreams. Return to mortal worlds."

This was easy for her to say, but every time I tried a new pain intervened. Wherever my dreams were, the gods that ruled that world did not want me to escape.

I had to scream out for every inch I gained on the long, tortuous path which led back from stupor. I had to clench my fists and bite blood from my tongue while I drove the nightmares out.

"How do you feel?" she asked.

I stared up at the crone. "Who are you?" I murmured.

"My name is Grubok. I am a healing mage. I took it upon myself to draw the stings from you."

"What for?"

"Because your friend, the one with the auburn hair, begged me to save your life."

"She's my companion."

"I know."

"We are seeking something."

"Try not to think right now; try to regain your strength."

"What strength? What place is this?"

"The town of Bakkmalar."

"I've heard of it," I sighed.

Julivette touched my brow. "The poisoned bites have passed. Your strength will soon come back."

I said, "This nightmare—"

"The healing mage, Grubok?"

"She's hideously foul."

"She has a gentle heart."

"She's got a hand like bone."

"Her flesh was gnawed away by poison from Gaylor. The whole of Bakkmalar has been all but destroyed. Gaylor's men come for tithes, and drive their children off. They take them to the mines where Gaylor seeks gold to line his Death Palace."

I said, "The town's empty—"

"The people hid in fear. They thought we were a sign that Gaylor's men had returned. They hid beneath the floors, in cellars and alcoves. We walked right over them."

"I don't believe it."

"This town is dying fast. It has lost the will to live, and the people are like shades. They wait to die, too numbed by Gaylor's force to find the will to fight. He has destroyed them, poisoned their fields and crops. He's put corrupting herbs in their rivers and streams. He's dropped death into their wells, so that the water they drink sears their throats."

"Where do we come into it?"

"We don't. We have to leave because they fear that Gaylor will think they harboured us. They know we're from outside, and think we could be spies for an invading force."

"Us, spies?"

"They're frightened; their own shadows make them jump. These people have no soul, and they have lost their hearts, yet I pity them." She stood up slowly, and gazed around the room in which the old mage worked, which was little more than a cell. "I come from a warrior tribe, raised to praise courage. Yet I pity this town."

"This could happen to all of us."

"I know." She gave a nod. "The world is waiting now to see what Gaylor does next. If he destroys the Star then he will destroy us all, with Darkness at his heels."

"The Star?" I murmured.

"The townsfolk saw it pass. It headed to the west, slowed down by a sea of sand. They saw a second force – my Drang-mi-laran kin – ride in pursuit of it."

"So they are here, then?"

"They must have found another route, and will

be pursuing the Star, hoping we will follow. The townsfolk said they scoured the foot of the mountain in vain, hoping to spot our trail."

"They did not come here, though?"

"Briefly. The townsfolk hid. And now they've six days' start on us because of your illness."

"Will they give us horses?"

"Not willingly," she said. "But yes, they will give us two."

We thundered out of town on two skeletal beasts whose spirits kept them strong. They put their heads down and tore across the plain, raising ribbons of dust which lingered in the air. I tried not to cry out at the pain which filled my face, and clutched my mage's charm.

For several days we advanced through a land so bleak, it pressed down on the soul.

We followed dust trails, and wandered through grey hills. We rode over ancient bones which cracked beneath the horses' hooves. We sought out signs of life and found only signs of death.

Tired and disheartened, we felt our spirits sag beneath the putrid light which covered all that world. It niggled at our eyes like fumes from stale blood, and withered up our souls.

We were in a dead land whose life-force had been crushed by the invasive gloom which issued from Gaylor. We might wander for years and see nothing but doom and emptiness.

On the eighth day we gazed down from a grey spur of rock on to a dusty plain. There was a dark haze some distance to the east, where huge pillars of smoke rose up from belching mills. Dim flashes were flames from mighty furnace hearts, spouting up into the sky. We could hear thunder, or maybe it was just the wheels of battle carts as they rolled through the hills. We caught the acrid stench of sulphur in the air, and tasted bitter smoke. But the distant factories were not what held our gaze, for there were grimmer things out on that dusty plain. Finglor's band had found the Star bogged down in seas of sand, and was now engaged in fierce battle with the warriors who were accompanying it, as well as with two Dark Land patrols which had joined in the affray. Outnumbered six to one, the Drang-mi-laran force was being cut apart.

"My mother!" cried Julivette, as she drew her slender sword and galloped down the slope. I called to her to stop, for nothing would be gained by adding one more death to the toll, but she was out of range before I found my wits, so weary was my mind. She was brought to a halt when her horse stumbled, and she crashed from its back in a cloud of dust. Half-stunned, all she could do was watch the horse trot off, trailing a broken rein.

In a hollow in a grove of rocks we lit a small camp fire of ancient, rotten logs. "We could not have saved them," I murmured through the flames. "We would have died."

"Death is better than disgrace."

"We suffered no disgrace. The fight was not our fight; we were too far away."

This cut no ice with Julivette, and she gazed back at me with eyes black as coals.

"Nor were they all cut down; we saw half led away," I continued.

"Led off to slave camps, or to gold mines to work for Gaylor!" Julivette spat. "They were chained behind the carts like dogs. The Drang-milaran line will die in shame and pain, when it should die in battle." A deep sense of rage and bitterness was overwhelming her grief, and I hoped it would help her to deal with it. But then she continued, "We should die trying to set them free."

I was not too sure of that.

Picking up a brand she held it to the sky, like a slim, brave statue announcing her revenge. But in those empty hills, in that dead, lonely land, it seemed a forlorn thing.

I said, "We will die here if we challenge that Dark Land horde."

"Not if we raise a force so that we're not alone."

"There isn't time," I said, "and Moridor won't fight."

"The Bakkmalarans might."

I laughed without thinking. "A town of wasted souls? As you said, they're afraid of their own shadows. You'd have greater success trying to enlist these rocks. Bakkmalar will not rise."

"I liked them," Julivette said. "I think that they may fight."

"Oh, sure!" I turned away and snorted at the dust. "And fatted pigs might fly and dogs climb trees."

"Then Bakkmalar will die. Because if they refuse to help us they will crumble into dust, and Gaylor's Dark Land troops will dance on their graves."

"As they may dance on ours," I said, watching the thin dirt-clouds stirred by the departing carts.

CHAPTER 15

Sharing the one horse which remained, we made our weary way once more to Bakkmalar. Through all that dreary landscape we practised stirring words which we hoped would make the people rise up and rally to our cause, but underneath it all we knew such desperate hope was only wafer thin. The people of Bakkmalar had been terrorized by the Lord Gaylor himself, and it was difficult to see how they could react favourably to our plea. But we had nothing much to lose, and could but try our best and see where fortune lay.

As we passed through the town's main gates we sensed the weight of fear pressing down on Bakkmalar. The people thought we'd left them and they could rest in peace, but like some dreadful dream we'd come back to haunt their sleep. It was much like Moridor, where the people hoped to slip through life, until life intervened in unexpected ways. Alas, what we brought would ensure that Bakkmalar did not sleep well again.

In the main square of the town we slid down from the horse and let it wander off. We stood there waiting for the people to arrive, for the need for secrecy was over and they had no reason to hide. Sure enough, one by one they came to the square to see what news we'd brought. In silent clusters they waited in the dust, studying our weathered clothes, our tired and sombre looks. They checked the weary horse, and must have wondered what had become of its skeletal friend. But no one challenged us, and I felt that they had suspected we would return bringing bad news. So often when strangers arrive, they change the course of fate, like stones tossed into a pond.

When the square was packed we stood on a wall and spoke to the throng. We spoke of Gaylor, and the darkness that he brought. We spoke of the Star and the hope its light could bring. We said that Gaylor's plan was to destroy the Star, for light was what he feared. If Gaylor won now, then for the whole of time Darkness would rule the world, and normal life would cease. We said the power he feared was almost within his grasp, and endless gloom beckoned.

When we'd said all this we awaited some reply, but saw only empty eyes and mute, impassive mouths. They might have been deaf, for not a single soul responded to our cries. With some desperation I cried, "Sad Bakkmalar has tasted Gaylor's wrath, and fears he will come again!"

"And what do *you* offer?" someone yelled from the back of the crowd.

"Your town's revenge," I said.

After some long debate we were ushered into a room. Once a great throne room, the place had been stripped of its wealth and the walls were encrusted with mould. The roof, once lined with gold, was now nothing but a sieve through which the wind whistled. Two thrones stood there, but they were made of rock, and the carpets were of threadbare cloth. A guest-table stood by, supporting six clay flagons, thick with dust. There was nobody present, and so we wandered round, gazing through high windows onto overgrown lawns where once great fountains danced and children laughed and played. The whole of Bakkmalar was like a memory now, a place where ghosts might walk.

"You should have seen it once," a voice said at our backs, making us turn around.

In a wide, arched doorway stood an ancient woman, resplendent in a long blue gown which the looters had overlooked. She had once been tall and strong, but age and bone disease had left her bent and stooped. Her long white hair glittered in the light cast by the few small lamps which flickered on the walls. Her eyes had once been jade, but pain and weariness had sapped the strength from them.

"My name is Tellermere," she said. "Sit down and drink the dust." She gave a smile of bitter irony.

As we sat on stone slabs she limped towards the thrones, saying, "He will be here soon. It takes him time to rise."

"Who will?" Julivette asked.

"My husband Bobolop, Bakkmalar's former king. He is not a king now for there is nothing left to rule, so we merely sit and brood on former, better days. Does this depress you, youth?"

"No, ma'am," I said softly.

"Good. It depresses me." With a mighty effort the old woman crawled onto a throne, and spread her long skirts out so that they hid her feet. She rang a tiny bell which would once have summoned maids, but none came to her side. "You are not from Gaylor?"

"No, Ma'am. From Moridor."

"A town above the earth?" she said with some

surprise. "My aides never told me this. We seldom see such souls. You look a lot like us."

"Except that we are younger."

"Yes, half our youth has gone, taken to Gaylor's mines to feed his lust for gold." She gave a weary sigh. "Is that where you are bound?"

"I hope not," I replied. "We are merely hunting for something that Gaylor stole, a Star which fell to earth and offers life and hope. But our comrades were trapped and we saw many men slain. We need help to save the rest."

"Ah, yes," the queen said, "my aides told me of this. You want to stir this town to serve on your behalf."

"It isn't quite like that."

"How is it then?" she asked.

"More – it's more mutual."

The queen laughed, and her laughter was like a dry leaf scraping dirt. "You'll save our souls by showing us your Star?" she said.

"It will restore your pride."

"What do you know of pride?"

"Not very much," I sighed.

We broke off talking then, for a strange squealing outside increased with every beat of my uncertain heart. Something was drawing near, something which gave a grunt with every squeal it made.

"My husband Bobolop," said the queen, as a

wheeled and rusty chair inched slowly through the door.

The man inside it made the old queen look young; his years were so many they must have been beyond count. He was nothing more than a frame of bones, over which had been drawn a thin and yellow skin. His eyes wobbled like marbles in his face and spittle ran down his chin and landed on his chest. His bald head swayed and rocked as he moved slowly towards us.

"The King of Bakkmalar ..."

CHAPTER 16

The ancient king and queen sat on their cold rock thrones, gazing into our eyes.

"What do they want, Tellermere?"

"They've come to ask for help," she said, touching his hand. "They've come to offer hope."

"Hope?" Bobolop looked up. "For who?"

"For us," she sighed. "They'll give us back our pride if we agree to march out to die."

"Ha!" The king gave a laugh which rattled his bones. "What do they know of pride?"

"Not very much," she said. "We have debated that. They want to stir us to hunt a stolen star."

"A star? No stars down here, we know, for we'd be blind."

"The Star's beneath a cowl," I said, "shielded by lead."

"How thick?"

"Enough," I said.

This seemed to interest him, and the old king's head lolled back as he pondered on this star which had been brought to Dark Land. "Who stole your star?" he asked.

"Lord Gaylor's men," I sighed.

"Ah yes, it would be that. The great Dark Despot has run off with your star—"

"But we could bring it back with Bakkmalar's support."

"And what does that bring us?"

"The chance to thwart his plans. It's Bakkmalar's revenge ..."

In a dim room, in this city of the doomed, we ate a sombre meal. We ate in silence, while the warlords of the town conferred on the subject of raising arms against the Lord Gaylor. Though I title them 'warlords' they were old, broken men, almost too weak to raise their forks to their mouths. Their Battle-General was a man who'd fought before, and had his arms lopped off as Lord Gaylor's revenge. He was the only one who showed a spark of fight, except for Bobolop. They both seemed excited by the thought of donning weapons, as if their years of grief had left them tense inside and the chance to let it out was burning in their eyes.

Around the long stone table sat a horde of nervous men with downcast, haunted eyes. They were praying to die in peace, not to have death thrust on them by someone else's quest.

"What does it profit us to aid these smooth-tongued pups?" a blind lieutenant sighed.

"It aids you nothing," responded Julivette. "Except to bring the peace your souls have long been denied. You have been so oppressed you've lost the spark of life that makes a man a man. You've lost your children – you just let them go. You've seen your town pillaged, and did not dare to fight."

"What kind of talk is this?" the blind lieutenant screamed. "They come here scorning us!" He picked a knife up and slammed it down so hard that the thin blade cracked the stone on which the food was served. His fury crackled like lightning in the air, and thunder choked his words. "We don't need children to tell us what to do! We don't need *outsiders* to tell us where we've gone wrong! I say we lynch the pair and throw their bodies out to rot upon the plain!"

"And you'll keep on hiding!" shouted Julivette. "You'll keep on waiting here for Gaylor's men to arrive, wondering *when* he'll come, wondering *how* he'll come, wondering if you'll survive! He won't *reward* you for hiding in this town—"

"Take this abhorrence out!" the blind lieutenant cried.

"But I rather like the girl," Bobolop said softly. "The room seems filled with fire."

Julivette and I were left in a room little larger than a box while the town debated. There were two clear factions: those who were afraid, and those who saw a chance to exact revenge; those too afraid of death, and those too scared of life continuing as it was. The final outcome would also decide *our* fate, for without someone's help we would be a sterile force. We would have to slink back to Moridor with the news that we had failed.

As the hours slipped by we lapsed into a mood of sombre, tense silence. No matter what they chose, it seemed the way ahead would prove a painful road.

"We debated for several hours, until we reached a point where further talk was futile. Bakkmalar is divided," the queen Tellermere said. "The choice that you have brought has split the town in two. We cannot forge ahead, nor can we turn back."

I said, "King Bobolop seemed favourable to our cause."

"My husband's old," she said, "and has not much to lose. Others are not so sure; they think it would be wrong to incur Gaylor's wrath."

"So then, Lord Gaylor is the ruler of this town?"

The look Tellermere gave withered me to the core. "Don't try to shame me, boy!"

I said, "I shame myself. But we're in need of help."

"So say we all," she sighed. "What you are asking is that we go to war without a single soul fit to handle a sword. We have been to war before, and even fully armed and trained we were cut down. They took our children—"

"Then you have naught to lose."

"And we can bear no more since he poisoned the wells. Now, if Bakkmalar fights, it could be our last hour. Death waits at every turn."

Silence descended, until bold Julivette said, "Death waits for you now. You are slipping into it."

"But you're so young and brave," the queen Tellermere smiled. "And we're old and afraid."

CHAPTER 17

After two days of argument the doomed people of Bakkmalar voted to go to war. Clutching old pitchforks and the crudely fashioned clubs which were the only tools Lord Gaylor had left them, they gathered in the fields beyond the town's main gates, beneath their tattered flags. There were twenty-five thousand ill-equipped warriors: blind men with palsied wives and sick children at their sides, young men in frail wheelchairs which threatened to collapse before the next steep rise. Half-crippled horses were harnessed to the carts. Outriders on the flanks shielded their watering eyes. Bobolop raised his spear, but had to be held up as he threatened to fall.

Sitting tall beside him on an ancient dappled mare was the sad queen Tellermere, with Julivette at her side. But the queen did not look at her; her eyes gazed straight ahead at Dark Land's savage hills.

As we were so far behind the Star we decided that to follow its trail would be pointless, and we took a different route. Avoiding the wide plain across which the Star was borne we headed instead for the long, grey hills which formed its northern flank. The Star-cart itself could not be taken through those hills, so steep were the main trails. Also a mighty dust storm had gathered on the plain, and any advance through that would be at a crawling pace. We hoped to save several days, and intercept the Star some distance to the west.

"Julivette," I whispered, "those drums they keep beating will warn the Dark Land force of our presence."

As she reined in her grey pony she said, "We can't deny the Bakkmalaran force its final battle march. This may be the last time such a sound comes from their drums – it will die down soon enough."

"But we will not be able to take the enemy by surprise," I said.

"You think not?" she replied, turning round in the saddle to gaze back down the line. "Do you think that *this* army will not cause some surprise?"

She had a point, I saw. Who in their wildest dreams would think to meet such an unlikely force? Who would dream of going to war with an army which feared death no more than it feared life?

They looked quite terrifying in their unwavering stance. They looked as if they'd fight on when every hope was lost. These people had resolved to ensure that Bakkmalar's last hour would be recalled with pride.

On the sixth day of our march we reached a long, high ridge which overlooked the plain. Swirling below us was the dust-storm, raging still. Howling against our back was a strong wind from the north. Creeping ahead like ants was the straggling Dark Land force, battling through the storm. They had left their supply carts bogged down in shifting sand and struggled on on foot, with scarves tied round their eyes. A small band out ahead was their Drang-mi-laran prize, their present to Gaylor.

As we gazed down on them we saw a grey horse drop, too battered by the storm to take one more step. We could see scattered piles of weapons and spare packs leading back through the storm. The force was dropping everything in its desire to flee the plain and reach a clear plateau a short distance to the north. It had no idea that this would be the place where we would strike it down.

I crouched down in the lee of a crystal-dusted rock and slowly drew my sword. I had never fought before and would rather not fight now, but thought it hardly fit to watch while others died. That said, it was not hope or pride which filled my veins, rather a deep terror. I feared that I would either be slain or prove too weak to fight, and might let others down so that they would die in my place. I did not think that I could bring myself to kill, no matter what the cause. It went against my very nature. I thought fighters were fools, yet when I looked around, nowhere could I see fools. The Bakkmalarans were neither fools nor mad, and their hearts were nobler than my own. This was a point in my life where long-held beliefs were thrown onto the fire.

Yet still my instinct was not to raise a sword, and the weight which filled my hand brought anything but pride. This day would be the day when Callibar's ideals would be put to the test.

"Put your weapon away, Cal; you will not need it here. You have no need to fight."

I glanced up as Julivette leaned back against the rock, and I said, "Brave Bakkmalar prepares itself to die. I cannot just sit here watching them give their lives, while I toy with my sword."

She said, "They don't expect it; this isn't our fight now. They are fighting for themselves, to restore stolen pride. What we do doesn't count. It is for Bakkmalar that this day has arrived."

She made me look at them as they prepared to fight. She made me watch their eyes, which gleamed with pride and fire. She made me see the strength which flooded through old limbs, and made the crippled stand.

"This is their moment," she said, "their chance to live, their chance to wipe away the grief that Gaylor caused."

I said, "It's all so sad."

She nodded. "Yes, it is. God let them die in peace."

CHAPTER 18

The steady beating of a drum was the only sound to be heard above the howling wind. We were on the plateau towards which the dark horde marched, oblivious to our flags, too tired to see our force. Their heads were still bent, their cloaks were still flapping as they crawled from the storm. I tried to count them, and guessed at twelve hundred; ours was the larger band, but they were the fitter men. They were better equipped and better trained for this. All we had was our pride.

The one thing that puzzled me was that there was no sign of the Star, and no mighty iron cart came trundling out of the storm. But, in truth, my main concern just then was not for the Star; I was watching life and death.

On a rock whipped by the wind, the ancient Tellermere stood to address the throng. Her husband Bobolop was too confused to speak, so weary was he after the six-day march. He was propped in a chair beside the blasted rock, his great sword in his hands.

"Bakkmalar! This is our chosen hour!" she shouted. "We have sent out all we have to take on Gaylor's horde! Whether we live or die, none can deny the pride we have earned ourselves this day! The Despot's stormtroopers are spilling up this hill; the finest that he has, equipped with spear and sword. We'll show them what it's like to take on hands of steel and join combat with Bakkmalar!"

A great cheer went up from the assembled throng as young and old gave Bakkmalar's battle cry. And as I watched with awe, our ragged army poured down on the stormtroopers.

A ring of bristling steel sprang up as Gaylor's troops saw the descending throng. They threw up barricades of shields backed by their spears and placed a solid wedge of archers at the rear. They sparked a line of flame which advanced up the hill, scorching the withered grass.

But nothing stopped us: not arrows, nor flames. Every man who fell by the sword was replaced by another. Battling with staves and rakes, the Bakkmalaran wave struggled to force a breach.

I could hear screaming as Bakkmalarans fell. I saw the smoking earth vanish beneath the dead. I saw torn bodies crawl, desperate to strike one blow before their strength gave out. The Drang-mi-larans seized the moment and turned on their shocked captors, beating them to the ground and grappling for their weapons.

Mothers with children were fighting to survive. Old men with bloodshot eyes screamed out their old war cries. Bobolop, on his horse, with his sword strapped to his hand, spurred through the thickest throng.

"Fight, Bakkmalar!" he yelled. "This is our final hour!" He slashed down with his blade as a Dark Land general struck at him. He was swept from his horse, but struggled to his feet and strode on like a god.

Bobolop's sword was howling as he battled through the throng, making right for the heart of the stormtroopers' ranks. His wife fought at his side and, faced by such glory, the Dark Land troops fell back.

They'll never stop them, I thought. *They are too strong!* The strength kindled by the fight made them forget their years. Fury was in their hearts, courage was in their souls, bravery drove them on.

Then Bobolop stumbled as an arrow pierced his throat, and slumped to his knees as a second speared his chest. Tellermere held her ground, standing above the king, fighting to keep him safe. If he was about to die she was going to bury him, not see him dragged away by the forces of Gaylor. With anger on her lips she carved a swathe of death around her fallen love.

And other warriors went rushing to her aid, picking up fallen swords, snatching up glinting spears.

Right through the very heart of Gaylor's army they drove a wedge of rage.

CHAPTER 19

Flags fluttered in a breeze which scoured across the hill in the fight's aftermath. It brought with it a fine dry dust which cloaked the battlefield, so that a thin layer covered both the living and the dead. It sparkled in the eyes of fallen warriors, and in dead children's hair. The soft breeze whispered like a prayer for all the dead, and tried to soothe the pain of those who still cried out, but no breeze could erase the memories and dreams of the horrors I had seen. I had seen horses and children cut apart; I had seen proud men hacked down like bales of straw. I had seen an ancient king – the once-great Bobolop – shudder and breathe his last. And in the relative silence which now lay across the land, a tiny voice inside told me that all this was wrong. But what are men to do when reason won't suffice, and victory's required?

"The victory is yours, Tellermere," I said as the shocked queen looked around with anguished, haunted eyes.

"Not such a victory," she said. "It was a task which had to be performed, and we performed it well. We can return home with pride, but in regaining our pride we have sacrificed much else." She crouched beside me, wrapping her tattered cloak tightly around herself like a shroud. "And when Lord Gaylor hears of this he will have Bakkmalar destroyed, and my flesh stripped and hung."

"So don't go back there."

The sad queen gave me a smile. "No other place I know is more fitting to die in. We'll bury our dead here, then those of us who can will go home to prepare."

"You could come with us," I said, "and share the Star."

She said, "That is your rôle; mine is to finish here: to help prepare the dead, to say our farewell prayers, to leave our flag behind. We might be doomed now, but all who pass this way will mark how Bakkmalar fought Gaylor for an hour. They will see how pride and hope turned back the evil tide of Lord Gaylor's schemes and plans."

As she stood up, she handed me the clasp of her husband's cloak – a jewel-surrounded pearl. She said, "Wear this with pride, and say that you were there when Bakkmalar awoke."

As I watched the lonely queen walk slowly through the smoke of the battlefield, shame trickled over me. I had urged the Bakkmalarans to battle, and as such felt responsible for causing so much death. Our purpose had been to retrieve the Star and we had failed, for it was nowhere in sight. Remorse dogged my steps as I walked towards Finglor, who stood battered and bloodstained, with a captured sword in her hand.

"What happened to the Star?" I asked.

"There was some heated discord between the Darklanders. When the dust-storm struck us some wanted to head due north, while others preferred a route that circles to the south. It was felt that the Star would get bogged down in the deep sands further north, but since further pursuit seemed unlikely at that point, some chose to head direct for home, taking the shorter route. They brought us as their 'prize'. There's a bounty on our heads. Gaylor pays for human souls."

"So what do *we* do?" I said, looking around.

"We will continue to the north-west and hope to intercept the Star. Your friends are very brave," she said, meaning the damned.

I said, "They'll soon be dead."

After some rest I helped perform the grisly task of stripping uniforms from slaughtered Dark Land soldiers. Then our party donned them, strapping on metal greaves, slipping on thick back-shields of black leather and steel. We tried to make a joke of looking more the part than those we had stolen them from, but it was a very sick joke, and my new clothes smelled of death and tears. We then rounded up some steeds, and my uniform proved so cumbersome that I needed help to mount. But at least from a distance we looked like Gaylor's troops, and hoped that in that guise we could travel undisturbed. Close up, foes would see our eyes. They would see the blood we wore, soaked deep into our disguise.

For six desolate days we rode the lonely hills, hoping to find the Star. We watched grey vultures circling overhead. We choked on dust and ash brought by winds from the west. We scoured the rock-hard earth for signs of any troops which might have passed that way.

But we met nobody and saw no signs of life, until at last the empty hills ran out and descended to the plain. There, on the seventh day, we found the deep cart tracks which spoke of a heavy load.

* * *

"Finglor," a rider said, "a castle lies ahead. The tracks lead straight towards it and enter at the gates and, as far as we can tell, do not come out again. The place feels like a trap, however. Vultures roost inside the towers and wild dogs prowl round the walls. Whoever lives in there, I doubt they'll be the sort to welcome us with open arms."

Finglor said, "But you saw no soldiers?"

"I saw no one at all. It may be that it's an abandoned keep, but I suggest we do not risk approaching it."

"What *do* you suggest then?" Finglor asked. "That we ride around the walls and camp out on the plain? We are running short of food and the horses need rest, so I'm loath to pass by. More importantly, the Star may well be in there." She turned to Brizek, who always rode at his leader's side to help protect her from unforeseen attack. "What do you think?" she asked.

He replied, "I go with you. I always have."

CHAPTER 20

As we rode towards the gates silence descended over us like a shroud. The place seemed a shrine to doom, built to repel all foes. Its buttresses were claws, its entrance of black rock fashioned like a maw. The bones of nations were embedded in the stones, and eyeless skulls peered out as if scanning the plain. The wind which flapped our cloaks seemed like the breath of death, expelled from dry bone mouths.

As we got closer lightning flashed in the east, and thunder sounded overhead like drumbeats. The sky shrank out of sight, swallowed by the great walls on which grey vultures sat. Jackals were howling as the wind played through the skulls, and a keening, morbid wail issued from the stone maw.

We paused outside the gates and wondered who had built this place. None but giants could have worked on such a scale. No one whose heart was kind would build with skulls or decorate a wall with such evil designs. From every buttress faces gleamed – faces carved out of bone and painted with streaks of blood. Ancient, demonic runes were fashioned out of teeth, and nailed above the doors.

From every watchtower a corpse hung by a rope. In every high window a dead man had been wedged. On every patch of ground which fronted the great walls lay at least one crushed skull.

As we clattered through the gates into a vast courtyard, we caught the stench of blood. It filled huge pits like cauldrons made of stone, and the pits marked out wide lanes for travellers to walk. Guiding lamps burned on black poles and their soft, spectral light reflected from the walls.

We urged our steeds towards the inner gates, hoping to leave the stench behind, but it clung to our clothes and followed us inside, into a lamplit hall.

We clambered from our horses and led them by the reins towards the farther wall. There were six doors in it, and we took the first we reached, passing from a twilight gloom to a darkness black as ink. We stopped to make some brands from strips of Dark Land cloaks, and slowly walked ahead.

The place seemed empty: the corridor we trod was covered by fine dust which had not been disturbed. It was wide enough for carts, but we saw nothing there to suggest the Star-cart had passed.

Huge statues lined the walls, men of stone in attitudes of war. The helms on their heads were cupolas of bone and their hands grasped great stone swords.

Through each huge door we passed we saw more of the same: long gloomy corridors and statues carved from stone. We could hear distant sounds, but so vast was the place we could not pin them down. Faint sounds of hammering strengthened and then weakened, and then began again.

"We can't wander like this," said Brizek, "in these labyrinths of gloom. We could get lost here."

"We are already lost," said Finglor, "and every turn we make compounds our confusion. We should retrace our steps and wait outside the walls. How much lies beyond? I suspect that where we are is but a tiny step on a lifetime's journey."

"What of the hammering?" said Brizek.

"Track it down."

"It shifts fast as the wind."

"Quite so," Finglor replied. "We have been defeated here, and cannot hope to win in such an ill domain." She turned to the warriors who waited in the shade cast by the smoking brands and the great stone statues. "Turn and find the way back to the gates. We have no future here."

Thus defeated, we turned the horses round and walked back the way we'd come, recrossing wasted ground. The hammering went on. The silent statues watched. The choking brands burned down.

"Finglor, that gleam ahead is not a reflection of our brands – someone is carrying a light. A man is hurrying into that distant hall—"

"Then why are you still here, Brizek? Track him down!"

"He's vanished through the doors; he's – listen! Hear that sound? He's working in that room."

"Then go and find him before he disappears."

"At once," Brizek replied, springing onto his steed. Raising a cloud of dust he thundered down the aisle formed by the stone statues.

CHAPTER 21

The man Brizek had found mistook us for a force of Gaylor's desert troops. He was a tiny archaeologist, assigned to log the tombs which filled up several rooms of the castle. The tribe of giants had gone, but it had left behind a lifetime's work for men.

"Twelve years we've been here," the small man was saying, "and we have scarcely begun to collate the things they left behind. The sarcophagi alone fill ten massive tomes. See all these tombs here?" He waved his arm around the room. "This is just one family!" We saw a thousand tombs, enormous granite slabs covered with ancient runes and drawings of the dead. "All those stone statues are carvings of the dead. Those people *worshipped* death as other folk crave life." He beamed around our group and we smiled wanly back. He really loved his work.

"When we first came here some of the giants still remained. They were violent men, and cut us down like sheaves. One brigade at a time was sent to lure them out and kill them on the plain. That's how we got here, wandering round the plains and thinking, '*This* would be a good spot for a base.' What a big mistake that was! Do you know, a thousand troops died in the first three days? Of course you'd know that," he said, shaking his head as if admonishing himself for stating the obvious. "Military history must be far more your line than mine."

"Wonderful," said Finglor, "but if we could just ask—" The man continued his tirade. He must have lived a lonely life working amongst those tombs, and he loved the chance to talk.

"Of course, even after the plains wars many of them still hid out in the labyrinth of rooms under the keep. We had to work with guards standing at our backs, fearful for our own lives. My own tomb-teacher, a man of great renown, was ripped apart like a doll set upon by a pack of wolves." His small face looked bereft as his thoughts went winging back to those who had lived and died.

"Terrible tragedy," he said, as Finglor bit back

her impatience and frowned supportively. "It's never been the same since he went; others came, but no one's taken charge. They just take the gold and crack open the tombs, and there's so much of *worth* that we could learn from this. Do you know, these people had a god who came to earth and taught them how to write?"

"The other soldiers—" Finglor said quietly.

"Oh yes, your Prefect said you'd lost your brigade. They'll no doubt be in the old east wing - that's where we keep supplies for those who've braved the plain."

"Would that be far, friend?"

"You've not been here before?"

"This was our first patrol."

"You should have brought a map. People get lost in here."

"I know," Finglor replied.

"I'd better lead the way."

And so we followed him, this archaeologist who spent his entire life collating ancient tombs. He walked just like a bird, with tiny splayed-out steps, fluttering as he talked.

"Down here's where we first built the traps to hold the giants," he said, pointing at the walls.

I could not see anything except the high stone walls of a long corridor which ended in deep gloom.

"Portcullises of steel are slotted in the roofs, and freed by tapping stones. We used to lure them into a stretch like this, then drop the barriers down, trapping them in between. Then they were cut down with spears. I pleaded for their lives in vain – I thought we could learn much from them. The very last one died just two years ago – a great brute of a man, madder than wolverines. He was stripped to the waist and daubed with ancient runes he thought would protect him. They killed him right here," he said, touching a slab on which a dark brown stain remained. "Stabbed him through his great heart a dozen times or more. Still he came back for more."

"The Star-cart escort—" said Finglor.

"Just up here." The man pointed ahead. "Around the second turn." He beetled on ahead, his short bird-like steps skimming across the ground. "They will be carousing as troops are wont to do, and doubtless you'll be pleased to join them in their fun." As he spoke he turned around and grinned, then he tapped on the wall.

There was a moment during which nothing happened, then the stone gave a groan and slid into the wall and with a great crash of steel a barrier fell down to slam into the earth.

Another gate crashed somewhere behind our backs, and we knew at that point that we'd walked into a trap.

"I'm no fool," said the man. "I knew right from the start you were not Dark Land troops."

"You are from Moridor. You are a Star-Adept."

"Not really," I replied. "Just an apprentice."

"But you have some learning?"

"No, just a small handbook I'm to read on the way."

"This book reveals Star-lore?"

"Only the basic facts."

"I see." My captor frowned. He turned to the warriors of the tribe of Drang-mi-lar, who were so heavily bound they could scarcely draw breath. He said, "A Star-Adept?" but no one volunteered. They knew even less than I. This did not please the Captain who had led the Dark Land raid on my home and captured our great Star. Taking out a small knife, he stabbed it through the throat of the nearest captured soul. "It angers me that you've not brought an Adept," he said. "It would please Gaylor well if I produced Star-lore."

"You must be out of luck," Brizek said with a scowl.

He was felled with one blow.

CHAPTER 22

Guards imprisoned us in pairs in rooms below the ground. Julivette and I were thrown into a cell darker than any cave and stinking like a corpse, where we spent two fruitless hours searching for a way out, knowing there wasn't one. No one was fool enough to risk losing the prize of bringing up-worlders back to Lord Gaylor's home. The bounty on our heads was equal to many years' wages.

Gaylor wanted souls. He wanted *our* souls, to see how we would react to the chemicals and spells that his mage-scientists brewed. He wanted to probe our deepest thoughts in search of the Star-lore. For the great Star was a mystery even to my own guild, and no one knew where it came from or how its magic worked. All we knew was that it gave us light and radiated warmth, and might be sent from God. Because he was afraid of it Gaylor had left it till last, and pillaged all the world before turning to us. The Star was his greatest challenge, and if he dimmed its light Darkness would rule the earth.

"What do you think our chances are of getting out of here?" I asked Julivette.

"What do *you* think?" she said. "We're in a castle in the middle of a plain, and the castle's full of troops who are faithful to Gaylor. We're locked inside a room buried deep in the earth. Our chances are not good."

I heard her shuffling in the foul straw on the floor, and as she stretched her legs they pinned me to the wall.

"There is no hope at all until we leave this place," she said.

After what seemed like several hours a guard entered the cell holding a blazing torch. He said, "The Captain wants to have words with you."

I said, "He's very kind."

"Don't make jokes with him," he said. "He doesn't care for jokes."

"Neither do I," I said.

This seemed to confuse the guard, for he leaned

into my face and held the smoking brand inches above my head. I could feel the heat burning against my scalp. "I don't like you," he said. "I don't like folk who don't know when to cringe. You'll need to cringe – Broughdok will eat your heart if you don't play along."

"So I will cringe, then."

"Is that a clever remark?" The warder's grizzled chin thrust out towards my own.

"Leave it, Cal," Julivette said. "This man's not worth the time."

"You can shut up as well."

The big man was a paragon of courtesy and charm, and also smelled like a dog which has rolled in horse dung. I got up and followed him through the dimly lit corridors of the dungeon labyrinth.

At length I was ushered into the smoky room where Broughdok took his meals. He was sitting at a table where a heaped plate of meat gave off a sickly steam. It seemed barely cooked, and thick puddles of fresh blood surrounded it. His great bloated gut poked out between the folds of his dark brown robe and his black hair had been slicked back, lumps of fat and grease showing in its tangled curls.

"So you're not a Star-Adept?" he said, not watching me, and chewing on the meat.

I muttered, "No, sir."

"What are you then?" he asked.

"I merely came along to make the numbers up."

"Perhaps some hot coals will help you remember the truth," he drawled.

"Honestly," I murmured, "I merely came along."

"A youth from Moridor, who bears the Star-guild sign?" His eyes fixed on my own, and they were black as night.

"It's just coincidence."

"There's no such thing." Broughdok grabbed a hunk of meat and sucked it from his hand. "You came to tend the Star in case something went wrong on the long journey home. I'm not a fool, boy —"

"I never thought you were."

"And I am curious to know more of the Star. I wonder why it is that Gaylor rates this prize more highly than the rest. We had special training before we were sent for it – ways of containing it in case its shielding slipped. But what if it *did* slip free? What if my men saw it? What would happen?"

I said, "At first it would just make them blind, but within several hours it would destroy their minds. The Star gives off a power which wipes out human cells. They would become imbeciles."

"So it is like the radiation which sometimes comes from rocks?"

"Something like that," I said, "magnified many times."

"I have never seen true light. I have only seen the glow which comes from *our* dim stars. What does it look like?" he said, shoving his plate away and wiping strings of grease from his hands to his hair.

I said, "It shows the world."

"And how does your world look?"

"Darker with every day."

The Captain nodded. "I think you are very clever, and I also think you know much more than you'd like to profess. Could I master the Star?"

"I doubt it," I replied.

"Could you?"

"Given a thousand years."

Broughdok stood up, belching and loosening his belt, and stared towards the fire, gazing into its heart.

"Does that look like the Star?"

"Not much. It's just a child by comparison."

"And yet it burns so fiercely."

Lapsing into a reverie he waved me from the room, and the gruff, discourteous guard shoved me back to my cell, kicking me in the rear before he slammed the door and darkness reappeared.

"What did he want to know?" Julivette asked softly.

"He wants to see the Star. He wants to test it and try to measure its power."

"Would that be possible?"

"If he's prepared to die."

As I settled in the straw alongside Julivette I thought we might all die.

CHAPTER 23

The next day half a platoon of Broughdok's toughest troops loaded us onto a bamboo cart. With clubs and bullwhips they forced us to lie down, then shackled us with chains so that we could not move and covered us with a protective sheet. For we were going on a long journey through Cerilbongomar, the land of dust and heat which runs a thousand miles. We were to accompany the Star to the Death Palace of Gaylor, to tell him what we knew. Since our group was unlikely to cooperate willingly in this, the soldiers told us many times of the tortures we would endure. Having our souls ripped out seemed the very least of what lay in store for us.

* * *

After twelve hours of travel over the plain the convoy made camp beneath the spectral 'stars'. We were exhausted by the heat which rose from underground and almost cracked the rocks. There was no night's relief, no dark to kill the sun, for the light was not sun. The dry ground seared us when we were let down from the cart, and we sweated like pigs although we wore few clothes. When water was brought around in a tank hauled by a cook we lapped it up like dogs. We had no thoughts of escape, for we were too worn out. The guards released our bonds, then handed out thin sheets of grey cotton in which we wrapped ourselves. We slept restlessly, tormented by dreams which showed the days ahead and tortures at their end. Our quest to save the Star seemed to have died on Cerilbongomar ...

"Wake up!" the sword-queen hissed as she pulled back my sheet and gripped me by the arm. "We have to talk."

"Of what?" I said, still only half-awake and not sure where I was.

"Of the killing of the Star. Of how to dim its light. How much do you know of it?"

I murmured, "Nothing, for we have not been trained for that. We are to preserve the Star, that's the whole purpose of our guild; to keep it safe from harm and ensure that it endures for as long as we endure."

"So it cannot be dimmed, then?"

"I don't know, I suppose it could. But I'm not the one to ask; you'd need a full Adept."

"You are not lying to me?" said Finglor, gripping my face so fiercely that I squeaked.

"Why should I lie to you?" I said, shocked and afraid, for she was so close now I could hear the creaking of her greaves and feel the heat which rose from her muscled forearm.

As I tried to squirm free her hand tightened like a vice, and she said, "To save your life at the expense of we Drang-mi-lars. To have a bargaining point, and give the Lord Gaylor the thing which he most craves."

"That's crazy!" I said "I'd never hurt my friends!"

"People do desperate things when torture is at stake."

"On my dead mother's life, I swear I have no clue how to dim the Star."

Finglor's grip loosened after a moment's thought. The blood rushed back to my cheek and I rubbed at the spot.

She said, "It is as well you don't, for I would cut your throat to keep you from Gaylor."

I think she meant this in some kind of positive way, but it was hard to sleep again after she had slipped away. My dreams were filled with spurting blood and visions of Gaylor.

The next day the brigade moved on like a horde of beaten troops, defeated by the heat. If Broughdok felt victorious at his capture of the Star his pleasure was soon sucked out by Cerilbongomar. It was a trek through Hell, where every breath was hard and every step a chore. Of course, our group was spared the worst of this as we were carried on the cart, but the Dark Land soldiers soon ensured that we paid for our luck; they tore away our sheet and half-emptied the tank where our water was stored. With tongues like cloth balloons we watched the water drain into the bone dry earth and then evaporate.

With the loss of water came the risk of hallucination, and each time I peered ahead the patch of gloom I saw seemed to have moved closer still. I was not the only one to see it, moreover.

"That patch of gloom ahead," I heard Broughdok murmur, "what do you think it is?"

"It could be a cloud of insects," said the Captain's first-lieutenant, who had been studying the gloom through a brass telescope. "It's rather hard to tell at this range, but I think it's an insect swarm."

Broughdok gazed down at him from his massive chestnut mare. "There are no insects here," he remarked, "there's nothing for them to feed on." He extended his left arm, and said, "Give that to me, I'll take a look myself."

Raising the brass tube to stare across the plain, he focused on the cloud which hovered in our way. "You might be right," he said. "Send a detachment out to check it and report back."

"At once," said the lieutenant, and he turned his horse away and sent out seven men to check on the strange cloud.

When none of them came back he said, "Whatever it is, I think we should go around it."

Going around the cloud proved difficult, for it extended for miles. Every time Broughdok thought he'd cleared it another swarm appeared, and as we rode closer a buzzing filled the air. There was little doubt at all that what we saw ahead were insects on the march. They were shuffling towards us like an army of black specks, some crawling in the dirt, some drifting on the air. The consensus of the brigade was that they were half locust, half killer wasp.

It seemed that Lord Gaylor had once instructed a scientist-mage to transform all crawling things into a Dark Land force, but the experiment had gone wrong and several mutant breeds had been unleashed on the world. Most died out fairly rapidly, unable to reproduce, but some had disappeared amongst the plains and hills, and it appeared that what we were looking at was one of those rogue hordes.

"An extra month's leave for the man who finds a way to get us through these things." A frowning Broughdok looked round his small circle of aides, who stared mutely back. "An extra stripe to wear upon your sleeve," he added. Still they held their tongues. "A bonus of several hundred franks, a star upon your chest, a feather in your cap, a kiss on the cheek from any maid you want—" Still silence. In desperation Broughdok cried: "Does anyone know the first thing at all about wiping out bugs?"

"Use smoke," somebody said.

"A ten-mile stretch of smoke? What do we burn, the earth itself?" Broughdok looked round despairingly. Then, with a weary sigh, and wearing a resigned expression, he said, "Call out the mage!"

The brigade's spell-mage rode from the convoy's rear on an ancient grey ass. Wearing a long brown tattered cloak and bearing a huge pack he looked for all the world like a traveller from the past: a wanderer from the days when it was safe to roam, begging from town to town. When he threw his hood back I saw a mane of golden hair, high cheekbones, a narrow jaw and startling emerald eyes. When he spoke his voice was old and rich with time, yet his face was that of a young man little different from myself. I have heard that mages age more slowly than others, but he looked much like a boy against the worn and grizzled Captain of the Brigade.

"What do you want?" inquired the mage.

"Can you get rid of that swarm?"

"How soon do you need to know?"

Broughdok sighed patiently. "Now would be a help," he said. "That is, unless you have something more urgent to do?"

"No." The mage gave a frown and narrowed his green eyes as he stared at the swarm. "These things take time, though; I can't just march on in. No doubt that swarm was born in one of Lord Gaylor's labs. There will be as much magic as science in its genes, and magic is a tricky thing."

"I know that," said Broughdok. "That's why you were sent along, in case we needed you to combat offensive charms. I know that you mages think you're a cut above soldiers, but you still have to work."

The young mage nodded thoughtfully. "It's not the work," he mused. "It's just that if things go wrong this magic could backfire. Life can be hard enough without a miscast spell rampaging round the plain. If my destruction – say, bolts of Dark Land fire – were to bounce back from the screens of magic surrounding the swarm, we could be burned alive and become nothing more than dust on the plain."

"So what you are saying, then, is that you can't

do it? You can't defeat this swarm, and we're held prisoner here?"

"Not at all," said the mage. "It's just that it will take some time, and there's some risk attached to unleashing the spell. What I am proposing to you is that you use your troops to raise defensive walls around the combat zone, and I'll work from this spot, trying to field something to clear a path for us."

"Do you mean Dark Fire?"

"Something along those lines."

"I saw that fire used once in a campaign to the south. It ripped right through the hills and killed both good and bad, our troops as well as theirs."

The young mage sighed. "I must confess to having problems using it. Doubtless the gunpowder which Gaylor is working on now will take its place one day."

CHAPTER 24

For the next several hours we worked alongside the Dark Land troops, erecting earth redoubts. Through veils of sweat we shovelled the dust of Cerilbongomar, and hauled up its baking rocks. Though we wrapped cloth round our hands to shield them from the heat, the cloth soon smoked and charred.

When the first wall was completed we were instructed to fashion a second one to protect the huge Star-cart in case the spells went wrong. Then we raised a rough stockade to contain the snorting beasts of Broughdok's Star-brigade.

Like true slaves we toiled on while the young mage sat and hummed on a mat of woven fibre threads which he'd pulled out of his pack.

Surrounded by his vials, he seemed quite oblivious to us.

When our task was near-complete the mage cast his first spell, and it smoked into the earth.

He looked nonplussed, then reached down into his pack, pulled out two long bands of multi-coloured cloth and bound them round his hands. They burst into flame. Casting them sideways he stamped the blue flames out, much to the disgust of the watching Captain Broughdok, who was muttering helpful remarks such as, "I'll skin your bones if you don't work this out!"

Next the mage found some candles, and stood them in a line supported by small piles of fine-grained silver sand. He shouted at the sky and offered up a dance of stiff-legged, clumsy steps. Then he stumbled backwards as the candles shot out flames which formed themselves into a ball of fire and rolled across the plain. He stared in disbelief as it trundled through an arc, then went back the way we had come.

After a pause, Broughdok snorted, "Have you done this before?"

"Not for some considerable time, and then it seldom worked. It's all to do with lines of force within the earth. Magnetism and such."

"Well, should we wait here or go back to the castle and rest?"

"No, I should have it soon. It just needs one more step."

Broughdok sat down on a rock, put his head in his hands, and stared at the dry, grey ground.

The final casting of the spell took us all by surprise, and threw us to the ground.

A crash of thunder was accompanied by a flash of lightning which at first sight appeared to have emerged from the mage himself. It flung him onto his back and writhed about his hair, then set fire to his clothes. Shrieking and writhing, he clambered to his feet and snatched up a brand. "Burn! Burn!" he cried as he charged towards the swarm. Sparks shot out of him as flames embraced his arm, and the long brand smoked and glowed and at last burst into flame. It tore free from his grasp and plunged into the ground, crackling in the dirt. With a mighty roaring the grey dust fused and cracked, and a huge orange flame burst into life. Thundering like a storm it advanced across the plain, heading for the swarm.

With a great cry of triumph the mage punched the air, ripping his torn cloak off and dashing it to the ground. He clutched his streaming hair, thrust out his chest with pride, and waited for applause.

But there was silence, for something had gone wrong. The fire wiped out the swarm but then refused to die. It hovered on the spot, and long dark cracks appeared in the plain's dust.

Someone cried, "What's happening?"

The mage said, "It's backfiring. I rather feared it would – we'd better take cover."

With looks of alarm we crouched down in the dirt as the earth began to shake.

"Is it over now?" Broughdok said.

"I'm not sure," said the mage, looking worried. "It could still be gathering."

"What could?"

"A counter-thrust. I've provoked Gaylor's spells, and they may turn on us. The magic that he wove into those bugs and drones will seek to take revenge."

"Then we'll increase the height of the barricades," said Broughdok, thinking still in the pragmatic terms of the military mind.

"That may not be enough. Judging by the weight of static in the air his power was too strong and has outperformed my own."

"Are you saying that we're about to face one of Lord Gaylor's spells?" Broughdok raged.

"Only the hidden charge: the self-destructive force which outlasts the design. It's like a bonfire which keeps a searing heat within its embers after it has burned down. Given sufficient fuel you could provoke that heat to light a second fire."

"Then don't provoke it!" Broughdok cried angrily. "Let it fizzle out!"

"I fear it is too late for that." The mage shielded his eyes as something on the plain blossomed and took on shape.

The whole brigade scattered as the demon in the core of Lord Gaylor's spell appeared. Amidst peals of thunder it took form on the earth: a towering wall of flame with werewolves at its heart. In colours plucked from Hell it writhed and chewed the dirt, spiralling like a coil. We were flung backwards as tremors rocked the ground, and lightning from the coil flicked out great tongues of fire. The horses, scared to death, crashed out of their crude paddock and thundered across the plain.

In scenes of pandemonium soldiers pursued the beasts, or drew their long broadswords to fight the black werewolves. The Star-cart gave a lurch as its horses bucked and reared, then tore off to the east.

With yells and screaming, death strode through the brigade's ranks, cutting down friend and foe and all who might resist. But we had no swords and our wrists were chained. We could only run and hide.

CHAPTER 25

For almost thirteen hours the spell raged on the plain, battling the Star-brigade. Its tongues of lightning and its vicious blades slashed through the thin defences of the desperate bands of men who fought with stubborn pride and all the skill they possessed, only to be cut down.

As they retreated grudgingly before the spell's advance we picked up blades ourselves and drove them through our chains, but there was little we could do but fall back alongside the embattled brigade. With werewolves harrying us and lightning all around we inched across the dead which now littered the plain, fighting until the spell ran out of rage and power.

We wept from weariness and shock at what we'd seen. We wept for all the dead and wounded of our band. We wept for our own lives which had somehow been spared. We wept, or else we screamed. For there was a nightmare of terrible carnage lying across the plain: dead horses, roasting flesh, torn clothing, tongues of flame. The smell of burning men hung heavy on the air of Cerilbongomar.

Julivette touched my face and said, "Are you all right?"

I nodded. "Still alive."

She threw her sword down, wiped blood from her hands, and said, "Half of our number's gone, and we're now down to fifty-five. The Star-cart's disappeared, and the surviving Dark Land troops are scattered on the plain."

I said, "What of the Captain?"

"Broughdok has been destroyed. Finglor's found their mage, who's in a state of shock. Brizek is gathering swords and salvaging what he can. We've captured several steeds."

I said, "I rather liked him."

"Who?"

"Broughdok. In a way."

She said, "Don't be deceived; he had a heart of stone. All Dark Land troops must swear a vow upon their lives to serve the Lord Gaylor." Then she pushed her hair back and stared across the plain. "Finglor believes the Star has gone for good," she said. "She thinks we won't catch it, and the only hope we now have lies in the Death Palace."

"The Death Palace!" I cried.

"That's where the Star will end. That's what it's all about, and always has been from the start. The fight between Light and Dark will take place within the halls of the Lord Gaylor himself."

Julivette picked up her sword and said, "Collect your things. Gather up what you can and be prepared to march. We head directly north, into the very heart of Gaylor's black empire."

PART 2

CHAPTER 26

As we proceeded north a land of hail and ice replaced the scorched desert. A gale twisted around us, sharp as lizards' teeth, and thick cushions of cloud concealed the blood-red sky. The only light there was came from the frost which glimmered on the rocks. We were as cold as we could be without freezing to death, and wrapped ourselves in the pelts of the beasts our archers killed. They brought down fox and elk, a pair of starving wolves, two deer. But even these thick skins failed to keep out the wind which whistled down from the hills.

Despite these hardships, though, I had made another friend and I was sore in need of friends at that grim time. With the exception of Julivette, I sensed the Drang-mi-laran warriors viewed me as spare baggage, a mere outsider who happened to have tagged along. Whatever use I might be had not been revealed to them yet, so they were polite – even friendly at times – but were never going to accept me as one of their own. If it were not for Julivette I might have groaned with pain, for I had grown to miss Moridor and the security of my home.

However our new recruit, the blond-haired Dark Land mage, was, as I had surmised, the same age as myself. As we were both from outside, we shared a mutual bond which drew us together. His name was Angridor and he had charm and wit, though whatever loyalty he possessed seemed a short-lived affair, for he had already denounced the Lord Gaylor and now professed himself eager to work with us. Like myself, he had become caught up in events that were far beyond his scope.

I would have been even more friendly towards him if I had been less intent on keeping the sluggish blood coursing through my frozen veins. It was difficult to talk freely when every breath I took hauled frost into my lungs.

"That quiet girl Julivette, are you partner to her?" he asked me at one point.

I grunted, "Partner?"

"The one who makes her sigh. The one who takes her heart and makes it laugh and cry."

"I doubt it," I replied.

He nodded. "Then in that case I shall try for her myself."

"Are you crazy?" I muttered, turning to stare at him through the veils of hail and sleet which slanted past our eyes. "Just because I'm not there yet doesn't mean I've given up on making her like me."

"Yes, I thought so," he said. "I thought I saw the signs."

"What signs?"

"The mooning eyes, the blushes and the sighs."

"What mooning, blushing eyes?"

"Don't worry," he whispered, "your secret's safe with me." Then he spurred his horse away and it slid across the rocks and almost dislodged him as he galloped up the line.

It was a short line which grew shorter all the time, for this quest was to decimate my new tribe.

After six days spent on the ice we descended through a layer of frozen cloud to a landscape of bare rock. All that we could see was mile upon mile of stone. Not one vestige of life dared show itself above the ground. No wild dogs prowled the earth, no vultures patrolled the sky, nothing gave out a sound. The only thing of interest was the outline of a town built on the shores of a long black lake of erratic design. The lake, contained by a wooden dam, flooded the jagged heart of a vast open mine which had decayed with time. Those sights apart, it was an empty land: a desert just as bleak as Cerilbongomar. Whatever Gaylor found when he fled into the Dark Land, it was not company.

"You know that every town will be aware by now that you are in this land?" said Angridor. "A band low on supplies can't get by on thin air. You're going to have to trade or steal at some point, Cal; Gaylor's still miles away."

"Ah, but we have an advantage," I said as I steered my horse around a black hollow blasted into the rock. "We wear the brigade kit and bronze insignia of the soldiers of Gaylor."

"That may not always help you in outposts as remote as this," he went on, "for not all are proud to say that they toil beneath his yoke. Gaylor conquered this world with promises of gifts which seldom materialize. He rules by force, Cal, and there are always those who will oppose that force by whatever means they can. A party of his troops taken far from the major routes – that would be quite a prize."

"You mean they might well kill us?" I said, gazing ahead at the small, lonely town which now seemed rich with threat. My spirits, low enough before, plummeted further.

"Not me, I think," Angridor said, "since I'm a time-served mage who still commands respect from superstitious minds. But for you and the rest this will be a major test of how much God likes you."

I said, "You mean we're idiots to ride into this town?"

Angridor gave a shrug. "I would have doubts myself."

"Have you told Finglor yet?"

"Not yet; I don't think your leader trusts me. She thinks I'm feckless and fickle, and a fraud who would sell my own soul if it helped to keep me alive."

"And are you?" I asked.

He shrugged.

Our band debated long on Angridor's advice as we reached the outskirts of the town. But as a virtual newcomer his views bore little weight, and I alone had any faith at all in what he had to say. It was indeed only my new-found friendship which made me look for wisdom in his words and kindness in his soul. Deep down, I knew we should ignore him.

In despair, Angridor made one final attempt to sway the warriors. "Ask yourselves seriously," he said, "what would it gain me to have you make a detour around this mining town and head directly north? Do you think I have a plan to kill you in those hills? Have I a host of men hiding behind those rocks? What possible reward could I gain if you bypass this place?"

"You could starve us," Brizek said. "Another week out here and we should be dead as the dust we grind underfoot. It seems to me that you have a lot to gain by keeping us away from fresh fodder and supplies."

"Fresh fodder out here, in that forgotten town? If those people had mules they would be long gone. The people in these parts are pretty strange, you know. They don't like strangers much."

"But you're a stranger!" Brizek said angrily. "Why should we rate your word above the things we need – food to placate our guts, fodder to feed the beasts —"

"Brain cells to fill your brain!" Angridor turned away, frustrated. "I've tried to help; I've tried to keep you fools from making a big mistake; but if you need proof, ride on into that town and see how long you last. And when they kill you, re-member what I said: remember that it was me who told you what they'd do. And when you go down to Hell think back to Angridor, and mark this lesson well."

"Don't lecture *me*, boy!"

"Oh, go milk a mule!" Angridor turned away, and sat down on a rock.

As we rode towards the town I glanced back and he was still sitting there, staring after us.

CHAPTER 27

Looking every inch like a lost Dark Land patrol, we advanced into the town. Children fled from us as we rode through narrow streets in which our horses' hooves stirred up thick plumes of dust, and brooding eyes watched as we cantered past low buildings cloaked with grime. Every dark, sullen eye glowed with the fire of rage. Of the few towns I have known, this was by far the most unwelcoming.

As we progressed further the anger took shape in the form of snarls and sneers and foul abuse. We had to grit our teeth as we rode through a hail of filth and saliva. Our brigade uniforms failed to provoke respect; if anything they provoked a greater hatred. Maybe Angridor had not been spinning a yarn when he warned us of this.

Finglor reined in her steed in the main square of the town, and stopped a passer-by. "Which way to the taverns?"

"Your backside shows the way."

"Another way than that," she said with some patience. Then she leaned down from her horse and gripped the small man by the throat. "Politeness can be cheap."

"That way," the man said, scowling and showing his teeth as he pointed to a gloomy lane. "Doubtless one of the cheap hovels there will be prepared to serve such Dark Land scum as you."

"Maybe we are not from the Dark Land," said Finglor.

The small man wrestled free and curled his palsied lips. "You're just in fancy dress then? We thought we'd seen the last of the leeches of Gaylor."

"We are deserters."

"Yes, sure, and I'm a prince!" He rubbed his throat where Finglor's grip had bruised the skin. "Just go and fill up your hides and clear out of our town. You're not welcome here."

Alongside Finglor, Brizek bristled at this open contempt of his beloved liege. I could see his calloused hand reach towards his sword, but

Finglor checked his arm. "Brizek, leave it," she said. "These people mean no harm; they are just not too impressed with the soldiers of Gaylor."

"Nor am I impressed with them," Brizek growled under his breath. "Some respect should be taught around here."

"Why don't we just purchase the things we need, then ride on out of here?" Finglor suggested.

So we rode past the small man and steered across the square to the dark, narrow lane where the town's taverns lay.

We filled a squalid tavern with the creak of our leather clothes and the clink of our long Dark Land swords. We sat at tables so thick with grease that we could carve our names in it. We could have scraped mud from our boots without the slightest risk of worsening the floor. The greatest danger we faced was that we might scare the rats, and if they worked as one they could pose a genuine threat. Brizek spent quite some time striding around the room, crushing the fat rodents.

"Food and wine for all of us," Finglor said to a short, fat man who beamed like a waxen moon. "And we should like a night's accommodation."

"I think that can be arranged."

"Plus stabling for the beasts."

"That, too, can be arranged."

"And clean plates."

"That's not so easy, ma'am, but I'll see what I can do."

The man nodded brusquely and made to walk away, but Finglor gripped his arm. "Please tell me why it is that we are so unpopular here," she said.

The man appeared surprised. "You are a force from Gaylor – what did you hope to find?" he said. "A warm and kind embrace? A welcome with open arms? People do not forget what Gaylor caused."

"What's that?"

"The rise of the Monster."

That night Finglor stationed guards outside the gloomy loft in which we were to sleep. Sleep proved elusive, though, for the total absence of any sound outside the building had us all on edge. It was as if the entire town held its breath. We had the feeling that all the people were out there, watching us through the walls and trying to smother us with the concentration of their hatred. We dared not look outside for fear of meeting their eyes.

All we could do was hope that they would soon tire and leave us alone, but as the night wore on the pressure from outside grew ever more intense. At first there was only a slight sensation of pressure on the brain, but gradually the feeling took on more solid form, as if the wall of eyes had somehow coalesced into one mighty glare. This gaze seared through us, stripping us of our will power, and we could hear that the guards outside were wavering. But after a time the only sounds I could detect were the thunder in my heart and the pounding in my brain.

"Finglor, I don't like this," said Brizek, as he tried in vain to pull his sword from its scabbard. Sweat showed on his face as he wrestled with the blade and I saw his deep brown eyes gleam with tension and fear, and anger curl his lip. "They are cursing us with some malevolent trick!" he cried. "Or there was poisoned food heaped on those plates tonight! Stir yourself, Drang-mi-lar – the forces of this town have evil in their souls!"

And we did try to stir ourselves but were unable to respond, for our limbs were soft as silk and the power had left our bones. When we moved to bar the thick loft door we lacked sufficient strength to raise its steel beam into place. While we struggled with it we heard soft sounds outside, and grunts from our guards as they were swiftly overpowered. We saw grey shadows move and heard the surly growls of men on the stairs.

With senses cartwheeling I landed in a heap at the foot of a flight of stairs, while all around me fell captured Drang-mi-lars. Paralysed by whatever spell had been cast on us, we had lain helpless while robbers took our swords, bound our limbs and covered our heads with hoods, then took us from the tavern.

I winced as I was dragged across the stony ground of the cold street outside. Like a trussed-up chicken I could neither flee nor fight, nor could I make a sound, for my tongue was numb. I could merely dream of revenge as I felt myself hoisted up and shoved on to a cart. I was the first, and others crashed on top of me crushing my lungs and making it hard to breathe. Surely death could not be much worse than this. I was convinced that I was going to suffocate as bodies kept pressing down on my spine and tumbling into my face. The cart gave a jerk and I prayed the journey would be short.

After a slow and bumpy ride which lasted for half an hour, the cart creaked to a halt and I heard several other carts braking beside my own. Although we had been given no indication of what might lie ahead, I had little doubt that without the strength to fight or the chance to plead for life we would be helpless pawns.

Still hooded and tightly bound, we were bundled from the carts and dragged across rough ground. A wind was gusting, and the funereal tones of a bell came dully to our ears. A smell of molten wax, which I presumed came from burning candles, was hanging in the air. Somebody touched me, sprinkling me with an oil which seemed to clog my lungs with its sickly essence. Somewhere somebody growled words from an ancient prayer which spoke of rage and death. We were inside a temple of some sort, I surmised, though not inside the town – somewhere towards the lake. I could hear the lazy splash of waves against the lake's high banks, and a black tern's piercing cry.

With startling suddenness our hoods were ripped aside and we found ourselves in the heart of a cold, granite temple lit by tall, flickering brands. Statues loomed over us – doubtless the miners' gods – and priests in long black robes chanted solemn anthems. The guards who lined the walls were not men trained for war, but they held their weapons well.

As I felt my strength return, and my escort let me relax, I sensed that I was being watched. The inner sanctum stood directly in our path, but it was wreathed in shade and smoke, like a great, fuming void. So intense was this shade that one would scarce have seen the Star itself had it been there. Yet the shade was occupied by something sitting on a throne, something that I could detect through a sense other than sight, and it was watching us with hungry, burning eyes.

We stood for what seemed like hours in the cold and lonely gloom at the heart of the stone temple. A stiff breeze blew on us, for the long walls of the nave were pierced at intervals by wide, open archways which looked out onto the rock from which the town was built and the great lake beyond. The lake was seething as the wind whipped the waves into huge spires of white foam. It was like a beast cursed with a thousand tongues, each of which lapped the air. And though I did not understand how, I sensed that all this rage was born of the dark void which swirled before our eyes. Whatever sat and watched us filled the lake with anger. The white tongues were its spite.

A voice spoke from the void for some time before I recognized what it was. So soft and low was it that it appeared to be the wind whispering around my ears, but what it lacked in force it compensated for with its sinister intent. For the voice spoke of tragedy and the offering of a life as payment for a life: a ritual sacrifice. It spoke of distant gods who had travelled to the earth and settled in these hills. The gods had wandered into a secret cave in which they had been trapped by agents bound to Hell; and as the gods decayed and their vast powers declined, entropy claimed their will. In a desperate compact they laid a bitter curse upon the entire land, and the curse took the shape of a beast of terrifying force, which hungered for men's blood. The cave held it trapped until the miners' shafts extended so far down that they probed beyond the rock, and then the beast was freed to terrorize the town, which had become enthralled.

"What has this to do with us?" Finglor uttered boldly, cutting short the soft words. "We are not your enemies – we don't support the beast."

"The beast hungers for blood," the voice said from the void. It was richer now, deeper and more rounded, with a harsh, husky edge. It was also closer, and something appeared to move within the swirling haze of the dark inner sanctum. A point of muted light was pulsing like a heart, and expanding with each beat. As we stepped backwards, almost against our will, a thunderous report made the whole temple shake, and the void disappeared as if it had been sucked into a monstrous maw. A fierce light blazed in its place and in its dazzling heart we saw, sitting on a throne, a woman dressed in flame, a woman scorched by fire.

"Witch Mandrigor!" screamed the priests.

"Tell me," said Mandrigor, "why you are proud to serve Gaylor."

"We are not his servants," Finglor said dispassionately. "The uniforms we wear were stolen from our foes. We travel through this land on business quite opposed to Gaylor's twisted goals. We seek to harry him on the route which he now follows."

"A route greatly removed from the paths which pass through here. I find it hard to see what you can hope to gain by roaming in these hills."

Finglor said, "A route to the Death Palace from the desert to the south. From Cerilbongomar —"

"That wasteland of dry dust! Nothing with good intent emerges from those plains. None but Gaylor's black hordes."

Finglor said, "Do we *look* to you like the servants of Gaylor?"

The witch spat out a laugh, which cascaded with sparks. She tossed her golden hair back and her sapphire eyes flickered with bolts of fire. Picking up a dancing flame, she crushed it in her hand, and thin slivers of fire crept through her long fingers. She said, "This flame does not hurt me, for I am rich with pain. Or perhaps it only appears so ..." She opened up her hand and the blue flame had vanished, and unscorched skin remained. "Perhaps I weave a spell which lets me touch your eyes, telling them what to see. So it may be with Gaylor, who might transform Dark Land filth into what some would see as wanderers from up-world. Is that what you pretend? That you are from above? I don't think so," she smiled.

"Then test us," Finglor said.

"I am not here to make tests," the witch said. "I am here to feed the beast which lurks beneath the lake; the beast which was released when Gaylor forced this town to extend its deepest mines. Not content with iron ore he chose to seek for gold, and it was the conqueror's avarice which brought ruin to this town. It seems fitting that those who wear his clothes should now appease his curse."

Then Mandrigor clapped her thin hands and the priests dropped to their knees while the grim guards crossed their shields with the long swords they carried. The words she spoke next almost died on the breeze. "Offer the fools!"

We were dragged out through an archway to face the full assault of an ever-rising wind. A storm had gathered itself in the mountains to the east and now swept down the lake, bearing splinters of rock. We were peppered by a hail which came not from the sky, but from the land itself. And as the awesome wind howled the lake churned in its rage, sending tumultuous waves crashing against the shore. The ground beneath our feet shook as if God Himself was pounding on earth's door.

We struggled desperately to break free from our bonds, but the guards held us tight and forced us down a trail. The trail was straight and smooth, and led directly down towards a jetty on the lake.

"A star, witch!" Finglor cried. "We are seeking a star!" But the witch merely laughed and beckoned on the storm. Each time she clapped her hands a wave reached for the sky, then thundered down again.

In the Dark Land's constant gloom the fire-drenched Mandrigor looked like a star herself. When she threw back her head she issued tongues of flame. When she flung out her arms fire spurted from her palms. Each time she exhaled, a column of white light shot out to pierce the gloom. And as the witch's long cloak swirled, flames arced into the lake. As she shook her golden mane sparks cantered through the sky. I was in total awe of her. What the witch employed was a sorcery such as I had never seen, the kind of unleashed power of which mages must dream. If she came with us, we could destroy Gaylor, I thought, but instead she was about to watch us plunge into the lake to feed the miners' beast. Far from being our great saviour, she was going to sacrifice us.

Guards wrestled with Brizek as he struggled to retreat from the edge of the stone jetty. They had bound his hands tightly, and now they were intent on making the loyal Prefect the first to feed the beast. They were trying to fling him down into the angry foam which churned across the lake.

Thunder was crashing, and lightning split the air. The witch's piercing screams implored dark, ancient gods. Finglor screamed back at her, pleading for her to spare the Drang-mi-lars.

But words were useless in the tempest which now raged about the priests and guards and Finglor's captured tribe. All talking was drowned out by the chanting of a dirge which was approaching its peak.

"Evil flee from this place!" Mandrigor shrieked at the sky. "Take these sad mortals' souls as penance for our own! We offer up these lives as propagating seeds—" and here the ranting witch paused. As she let her arms drop we saw her flames subside, and she stared past the startled priests straight into Finglor's blue eyes. She looked bemused, then frowned and pondered long and hard. Then, "What star?" she enquired.

CHAPTER 28

Finglor and Mandrigor debated long and hard, whispering furiously in the shelter of a wall which ventured a short way out onto the stone jetty. The wind, though still extreme, lessened a little as the witch relaxed her thoughts. Her cloak flapped and Finglor's jerkin creaked as their hands chopped at the air to emphasize their words. I sensed that change was afoot and prayed that the outcome would be in our favour, but the priests and guards looked tense, and worry filled their eyes as the tempest's fury died.

"There has been a change of plan," the witch said as she strode back to the waiting priests. "I have heard grave news which causes me some doubt, and for this hour at least will abort the sacrifice. I must have time alone to consider what I've heard and ponder on its truth. But if what I have been advised of is true, then I may have to depart this town —"

"Leave us?" a priest enquired.

"But not before I've told you the truth. You have been misled for a long time, I fear, faithful priests, and this may be the night truth will emerge. Until then, guard the prisoners well, for I must leave to ponder in my cave." The witch vanished into the hills with Finglor, leaving behind her a stunned silence.

This was the truth: there was no beast any longer. It had been killed off seven years previously when the miners dammed a stream and flooded their old mines in an attempt to rid themselves of the curse. But they let the curse live on by mystifying fear and elevating it, and continued to believe in the beast, even though it was gone. They still thought they would die if the beast should emerge. They thought the way to gain life was to sacrifice it – and they found Mandrigor.

Mandrigor was a great witch who had been driven from her home when she refused to serve Gaylor's twisted plans. She wandered the world, seeking some place where she might hide, pursued by Lord Gaylor, who feared her power. In this lonely land she planned to disappear.

By telling the people that their beast craved sacrificial flesh, Mandrigor ensured that any soldiers of Gaylor who might wander through the realm would be slain. The people did not know that she had lied to them – but perhaps they did not want to know, for then they would have no hope. Their mines had been worked out, and now they were flooded. Their only hope was to avoid the curse, and that became their goal. It kept them occupied and held them united. It kept their home alive when it might well have turned to dust. If they had left, the only work they'd have found would have been in Gaylor's mines.

There was a twisted morality at work here, which I could not quite grasp. Either the witch was wrong, or she was a perfect saint – I never could decide. What was clear beyond all doubt, however, was the deep hatred she bore Lord Gaylor. Mandrigor detested him for conquering her world and reviled his plans to corrupt the witch's art. She cursed him again and again as she recalled the names of wizards he had bought. It was treachery on a scale never known in the secret world in which sorcerers worked. She said that Hell itself would never have subscribed to Gaylor's grim demands. For his final purpose was to destroy all life and declare himself the king of a despoiled, murdered world. Then he would start again, building up life and men in his own accursed image.

"I cannot leave immediately," she said. "I must spend some time reassuring this shocked town. You go ahead of me and try to track down the Star, and I will endeavour to meet you somewhere on the road. If that fails I shall appear in the Death Palace itself – though that may cost me dear. Gaylor has set a price on the head of Mandrigor, and every blackened rogue will know my secret name. But if what you say is true, that you pursue a star, it would be worth the price. I could *destroy* him with a star – I could blind him." Her eyes gleamed as she dreamed of her revenge. "I'd penetrate the dark with which he cloaks his soul, and sear his twisted heart."

"We'll need the star back, though," Finglor said worriedly.

"And you shall have it back," the witch said with a frown, "as soon as Gaylor's dead. As soon as I've regained my place in this sad world."

So that was the deal, then: she would help us claim the Star and in return we would let her have it for one hour – one hour in which she would work to turn the Star's vast power into a destructive force.

As soon as our band had been re-armed, we rode out of town on our rested horses. We followed the lake shore to the lofty wooden dam, then took a winding trail down a steep-sided cliff towards a river bed littered with slabs of rock loosened by the witch's storms. The bed was wide enough to ride several abreast, for the river had run low, its force staunched by the dam. We rode with renewed hope, believing our meeting with Mandrigor to be a good omen. But there was still some distance to cover before we reached the mighty Death Palace of the Lord Gaylor himself, and the further we progressed, the deeper we advanced into his watchful realm.

After less than a mile we saw the figure of Angridor ahead of us. The young mage was crouching astride a slaughtered deer, ripping out its heart and making mystic signs. He told us he had hoped to save us from the townspeople and was about to make a spell. He seemed a little crushed when he heard that we had ridden freely from the town, but when we said that we'd had the help of Mandrigor, and sang her praises, he turned distinctly chilly and stalked off in a huff, muttering under his breath. It was only then we saw how much mage-rivalry there is in sorcery.

"I suppose she performed a *miracle*!" he yelled from a distant rock. "It's all a trick, you know—"

"Don't be like that," I said as I rode to his side. "She was only a sorceress who cloaked herself in fire."

"In fire?" Angridor appeared impressed, and

scowled down at the ground. "I couldn't do that stuff."

"But you do other things," I said.

"Like killing deer," he sighed. Turning to me with an anguished look, he said, "Actually I was trying hard to impress you with a spell, so that you'd take me along."

"Well, you can come along – we have an extra horse," I said.

"Is this one dressed in fire?"

"Not really; it's quite old. It mostly sleeps a lot."

So the young mage rode with our band towards the high, barren peaks which formed the last redoubt of Lord Gaylor's wasted land. When the time came to cross those soaring peaks there would be no turning back, for we would be within his realm.

We rode for several days, following the winding course of the half-exhausted stream. Nothing disturbed us, for all was still and dead. Barren rocks towered above us; long slopes of jagged scree and gigantic boulders were all that we could see. The whole grey land was silent, and the echo of our horses' hooves bounced back from the slopes.

By the morning of the seventh day we had abandoned the stony river bed in favour of the slopes. There we found an old and somewhat ragged trail – a former miner's track which speared between the peaks and saved us quite a climb. We stumbled across the miner's old tin lamp and a crushed cap thick with rust, but saw no sign of him. With every hour that passed we ploughed remorselessly into a thickening gloom, and the nearer we advanced to the empire of Gaylor, the dimmer were the 'stars'. This entire world was darkening, and the few crystals which still glowed in the black rock sky above seemed to be the last of their kind. Gaylor was killing them off; he was putting out those stars, just as he would put out ours.

The miner's track emerged through a narrow, steep defile on the far side of the range. Ahead was a barren wasteland, trampled and crushed by war, where the very earth itself was scorched by years of fire and outcrops of blasted rock thrust through fields of dust as far as the eye could see.

In the far distance, directly to the north, a line of smoke hung above the land. It came from weapons-towns where, day and night, foundries manufactured armaments and implements of war. They were forging mighty metal carts on which guns would roll. They were building beasts of steel which could withstand the force of an explosive charge. Gaylor was leaving nothing to chance as he prepared to launch one final, brutal assault which would destroy our world.

We pushed our horses on and descended to the plain. The air grew warmer, for it seemed the wasted land still contained the fires of Gaylor's war locked deep within its heart, and we had to knot thin scarves around our streaming brows to keep the sweat from our eyes. A dust cloud was hanging in the air, caught by the heat haze which shimmered above the ground, and the way ahead was soon obscured, as if we rode through smoke. We had to squint to make out what we saw, and sometimes felt we were not alone, but nothing untoward occurred as we progressed, and the mountains fell behind.

CHAPTER 29

After six days on the plain its loneliness and heat started to haunt us. We were growing desperate for a renewal of our supplies, and the water in our flasks was disappearing fast. Strange shadows lurking in the mist seemed to be closing in. We were stumbling like wanderers at the end of a weary trail and were no longer sure that we still followed a course towards the Death Palace. We felt that we might be marking out huge circles in the dirt, like targets for the hawks and vultures overhead. We felt we were being forced into digging our own graves in that forsaken ground.

"We can't go on like this," I heard Julivette say from somewhere in the mist. I tried to find her, but the swirling clouds of ash and the constant twilight gloom made it hard. My eyes felt red and sore, gritty from all the dust. I wiped them on my scarf.

"Where are you?" I said, and she whispered, "Over here ..." I turned my horse that way and spurred it to a trot, but I had to slow it down as a rocky outcrop appeared directly in my path.

"I can't see you," I said, as she murmured, "Over here ...", but when I tried again I encountered more rock. I said, "I think I'm trapped," and she said, "Stay where you are; I'll come and look for you." But she never reached me because someone up ahead cried out, "The Death Palace!" and thunder split the air. It was the roar of hooves and somehow Julivette became caught up with them. She yelled, "I'll find you!" as the horses disappeared through banks of roiling fog and shadows dense as rock. But she never did come back and my horse and I were lost.

I rode the empty plain for several hours, calling out hopefully, but no one answered, nor could I find a clue to where they might have gone, although the mist had thinned. All I could see ahead were miles of swirling dust and thrusting spears of rock. My only comfort was the horse on which I sat; the only signs of life were grey vultures overhead. It seemed that I traversed that plain with nothing but the breeze; but the breeze kept me company in a way that few friends have, for it did not debate or wander from my side. It merely tagged along, and every time I sighed I heard the breeze sigh back.

After another hour I found an empty flask, discarded in the dust. It was one of Angridor's: I could recognize it by the charms which the mage had carved on its side in an attempt to make it last. He had hoped to eke out life until we'd crossed the plain, but he had failed. It seemed clear to me now that we would never leave this plain on which so many had died during Gaylor's last war, and that the corpses lurking beneath that dust were waiting to greet my own.

I tried to shield my horse's eyes with a torn-off leather flap as a rising wind whipped up the dust. The wind had strengthened suddenly and was exploding across the plain in thunderous bursts of power. I could only grit my teeth and pray the storm would pass, while my beast struggled on. The horse had its head down and was shovelling through the wind while I clung grimly to its neck, flat on its back. In this sorry state we advanced at less than crawling pace.

Finally, the storm blew past and the weary horse plodded up a rising spur of land. For miles around us I could see open land unfurling like a chart dropped by a careless god. There were no landmarks to be seen – nothing but the deadlands of Gaylor. I had no doubt now that what my friends thought they had seen was nothing but a dream, some kind of phantasm sent to taunt them and lure them away through the storm. Even as my own eyes scoured the plain they could be locked in the cells of Gaylor's Death Palace.

"Which way would you like to go?" I murmured to the horse, who watched me from sombre eyes, still trusting that I would help him to survive. As I stroked him on the throat I prayed that I would somehow find the strength.

Another day alone at last brought me in sight of a black tower, thrusting up from the dust like an accusing finger. At its feet lay the ruins of walls which once stood proudly but were now heaps of stone across which lichens sprawled and vultures made their home, the haunts of sallow snakes with dead moons for their eyes and venom in their souls.

I let the grey horse wander free rather than take it any closer to the abandoned hall. I had heard from Angridor tales of deserted homes which were the haunts of ghosts and passageways to doom, where cellar steps might lead you down to Hell. I had never truly believed this, but when I got close to the ruins I saw bloodstains on the stones and fallen, shattered swords. One of the blades which I picked up bore clearly on its hilt the insignia of Finglor.

"Tell me," somebody had once said, "what is your greatest fear?"

I had said: "The darkness. A darkness so complete that it chokes your lungs and leaves your senses numb. The darkness you find in a room when the last candle fades. The darkness of a tomb sealed off against the world. The darkness of the dead."

Then the girl who questioned me (whose name I forget now) said, "What would you do, Cal, if you found such a dark?"

I said, "My heart would stop. I would freeze still as a stone. I would simply wait to die …"

Amid the darkness of the tombs which I had unearthed beneath the hall, I listened to my heart. It had not stopped yet and, in fact, beat like a drum, its every anxious note thundering out through the gloom. It pounded in my chest with all the shocked vigour of a bird trapped in a cage. So intense was this pounding that the blood-rush through my veins set lights before my eyes and I had to lean against a wall to keep from falling down.

My thoughts went back to a small room in the Guild, a cell below the stairs …

It was such a simple game we played, we children of the Guild, when each day's chores were done. Through the building's corridors and rooms we played at hide and seek while the Star's light was dimmed. Clutching long tallow wicks we would pound up flights of stairs, then thunder down again. I had never cared for the game but the others, sensing my fear, would make me play the hare and send me out alone. Once I hid in the cell below the stairs, where the darkness was so intense I feared they'd never find me. But they discovered me at last and they threw a dead hand in through the door without warning. I thought I would die. It was just an old dry leather glove but as I crouched in the dark, I thought Death himself stalked me that day. It took more than an hour for them to bring me round and stop me screaming. And when I look back on it now, I can see that it was more than the darkness which made me afraid; it was the pressure of being so alone and not knowing when my solitude might end and who might appear.

The silence in the cave of tombs was just as real as my room under the stairs. I had located the hidden entrance while gathering up swords my missing friends had dropped. Below a metal grille, a long flight of cold stone steps led downwards. There were signs of a struggle – bloodstains on the walls and gashes cut by blades as they slammed into stone. I had found a shattered helm and a rag torn from a shirt worn under chain mail. Someone had also died there: I had discovered a blood stain which could only have been made by a disembowellment. I prayed desperately that it was not Julivette.

How long those tombs had stood, silent and gathering dust, I could not begin to guess. They were so ancient that, even locked away from the corrosive air, they had begun to rot, spilling their contents through wide cracks in their sides. And yet I sensed that this was not the room in which my pounding heart would face its greatest threat, for there was somewhere beyond this place, further and deeper still, which I must find. The musty air here smelled too much of earth; nothing of flesh and blood could have tarried for long.

Groping around me, my fingers closed at last on the hinges of a second, smaller grille, and I struggled through it, despite the rising screams of protest from my soul. I continued to descend by a passage through the earth, so dark that it left me blind. Dirt sides closed around me more snugly than coffin walls, and the stench of clay hung heavy in my nose.

How long my journey took I could not say for sure; but it was several hours. I rested frequently, for the tense, dark atmosphere and extreme cold made breathing difficult. The gloom was thick and sour, redolent of stale air which had been inhaled before, and suggested a beast which, trapped aeons before, had festered but survived. Its heart could scarcely beat, its blood froze in its veins, but it was still alive.

Suddenly the temperature of the gloom began to increase alarmingly, and soon it was so hot that I began to fear the very fires of Hell itself blazed in the tunnel up ahead. I could hear a drumbeat, which might have been the pounding of my heart, and taste iron and steel, or the blood of my own lips. And I smelled roasting flesh and smoke as if, somewhere below, the beast of Hell scorched. I knew that if I paused nothing on earth would force me to move again, so I kept creeping ahead, while chunks of warm dry dirt crumbled beneath my hands.

At last I gazed upon a chamber lit by fires which blazed in great braziers. I counted twelve of them. Together with the brands fixed on the walls, they cast a lambent glow across the room's grey stones and the pools of blood which bubbled in the bowels of mighty black cauldrons. They lit on chalices and sacrificial blades. They flickered on thick chains welded to iron rings and bounced back from the tools which littered the floor of a vast torture chamber.

Smoke drifted into my eyes as I crouched on the narrow ledge of an iron-railed balcony. I had my sword drawn, though I doubted it would serve more use than a paper wand against the beasts below, which surely once were men, but now were so grotesque that they looked more like demons. Angridor had once told me that when evil dies it goes to Hell, where it is reborn in a new and twisted form, and what I saw below testified to his words. For I saw perversions, parodies of dead men whose eyes were crimson flames and whose hands curled into claws. I saw dry, peeling skin whose shade was only matched by bones on funeral pyres. I saw huge snouts which sprouted yellow teeth, and spittle which burned holes in the stones on which it dripped. I heard grunting and smelled corrupting flesh.

I crept back from the ledge and circled around the room through a low, dark corridor. I had seen my friends down there, locked in a cage, battered, bloodied and bruised and wrapped in heavy chains. I had also seen the black marble slabs on which the beasts were preparing to make their sacrifice. I was convinced that they must be devil-beasts, who offered up souls to preserve their own bleak lives, compelled to feed Hell's Lord who crouched on his black throne inside Hell's deepest hall.

As a hunch-backed guard appeared ahead I slipped into the shade of a twisted, black pillar. I thought he was sure to have heard me but he wandered idly by, so close that I could smell the pustules on his back and hear the rasping breath which grunted from his throat as he jogged down some steps. He must be going to join the hungry throng which milled around my friends and jeered at them through the bars. Doubtless he would lick his lips while he savoured the luckless brave whose dead flesh he would devour.

Desperate to find some way of helping my friends I crept into a room whose door-curtain was made of human skin. A black stone table and a chair made of lead stood there, and in a cupboard I found a vial of what looked like congealed blood. A bed supported a heap of the Hell-beasts' leather cloaks and rotting uniforms, but there seemed to be nothing to aid me. As I turned to walk away, a Hell-beast reared large in the wide doorway. I slammed him in the jaw with the hilt of my heavy sword, and he slumped down at my feet.

Taking the beast's sword, which was stouter than my own, I slipped out of the room and found myself once again in the gloomy corridor which circled the room of death. It seemed my friends were doomed to die, for I could not help them.

Once more I hid in shade while I looked down on the torture chamber. The slabs were ready now, and the time fast approaching for the first sacrifice to be dragged from the cage. It seemed that Angridor was to be the choice, and beheading his end. I had to do something, but the beasts were massed and strong while I crouched alone with my heavy sword. If the Drang-mi-lars could not fight off the beasts, what kind of hope had I?

I yelled *"Angridor!"* as the frightened mage was pulled screaming from the steel cage. His wrists were bound and he was kicking ferociously, but the Hell-beasts laughed as his boots glanced from their thighs. Doubtless they had seen often enough before how desperate men may fight when their turn comes to die. But my cry surprised them and every beast looked up. I had no choice now but to leap from the ledge.

Clutching the captured sword I landed on the sacrificial slab where Angridor was to die. For a startled moment everything seemed to freeze, but then things sprang into life and I went sprawling backwards, dodging a hail of blades. I knocked over a great silver cauldron as I landed in a heap, and pools of blood and fire spilled out across the floor. Somebody grabbed my wrist, and I slashed at their arm with the great iron sword. Then I started galloping across the crowded room, not sure of where I ran, but hacking all the time, and though I touched no one the Hell-beasts fell away from the long, scything blade. Then they began to regroup, and the hissing of blades drowned out my own.

In a desperate duel with death I battled through

a rage of sacrificial blades. Fires spread around me as braziers were upturned. Hell-beasts' robes caught light and voices shrieked with pain. The golden bowl I had snatched up to serve as a shield was battered and near-destroyed as axe blows swung in at me, clattering on the metal surface. Swipes from great swinging blades sent sparks out from my own. Blood spattered the walls as Angridor unleashed the spells he'd prepared for war.

A constant screaming rang in my ears. A haze of flashing blades dazzled my eyes. I thought, *This must be death; this is a scene from Hell.*

I was struggling to survive.

I reached the high steel cage and used a fallen axe to batter off the lock. I threw my sword in, and Brizek sprang on it and swung a mighty blow which shattered Finglor's chains. Then he cried out, and I turned just in time to dodge a flailing chain. I picked up a dagger and stood guarding the gate as the Drang-mi-lars poured out. With an almost indecent savagery they armed themselves with whatever they could and flung their pent-up rage onto the beasts from Hell, driving the monsters back. And as they overpowered them, they snatched up their fallen swords and kicked down more braziers. Great orange pools spread out across the floor, lighting up the grease-stained walls.

We battled our way to the gate which opened onto the shaft leading back to the earth. We snatched thick wall-brands to light the way ahead, and Brizek held the rear as we sped through the murk with the Hell-beasts behind us, filled with the rage of angry wolves. They were almost slobbering as they thundered in pursuit, spitting out their wrath through steaming, acid spray. Though we had come this far they still outnumbered us, and they were filled with hatred.

Brizek began weakening, and Finglor took his place. She too was beaten back, and others filled her space. One by one warriors stood, bravely defying the tide of fury born in Hell. Some were cut down and some brushed aside. Some were impaled on spears and some devoured by fire. But still our battle raged on, lining the long tunnel with the wounded and the dead.

"The gateway!" Angridor cried, and we surged forward with renewed hope. He cried, "Our freedom waits!" and we increased our stride. With the Hell-beasts close behind we charged into the piles of cold, abandoned stones.

Picking up their own swords, the Drang-milaran braves formed a defensive line as the maddened Hell-beasts approached, and in a terrible scene of death they waded through the throng, hacking to right and left. They showed no mercy, for this was grim revenge. I saw no quarter given, nor did I hear it asked. In the end I had to take my horse and simply walk away: I could not face any more death.

CHAPTER 30

As those who had survived the battle gathered upon the plain, Finglor came to my side. "Death sickens you," she said.

"It's obscene," I murmured.

She nodded. "And it's hard to justify the means."

I said, "The means are fine, it's the end result I find hard to explain. To watch you murder them—"

"As they would have murdered us, for if any of the monsters had survived they'd have planned *their* revenge. The Hell-beasts realized the moment they emerged that this was a fight to the death."

I said, "But we could have spared some – we'd proved our point."

"And what would that have shown?"

"That we have humanity. We would have shown that we're greater than them."

"Perhaps," Finglor replied. "But *are* we greater than them? All beasts are frightened and struggle to survive, and our humanity is an oasis in a vast, empty land through which our instincts stalk. We walk with animals at some points of our lives—"

"You play with words," I said.

"I have to bear the blame for how my warriors act," Finglor continued, "and this is not a game. This is the reality which you must face: that sometimes instinct wins and reason is brushed aside. Sometimes a darker force rears up to dim the light which blossoms in our souls."

"Just like Lord Gaylor," I said.

"Who lurks in all of us."

"So that at times we're all the same."

"Perhaps," Finglor replied.

I said, "I can see no sense in this, though I am straining to find some."

"There is none," Finglor said.

Amid the bleak ruins on the plain we covered up the dead with mounds of lichenous stone. We raised a flag to them and offered up the prayers designed to comfort souls as they drift through the void. Of those who had set out on the quest from Moridor, thirty-four now remained.

We had no horses save my old grey beast, which seemed increasingly to want to stand and rest. We loaded its packs with whatever we could save and headed northwards, leaving behind the ruins, and our lonely, tattered flag. We were staging our last attempt to reach Lord Gaylor's halls before death claimed us all.

"You are a hero, Cal," said Julivette.

"I don't feel much like one," I replied. "I never stopped to think that every soul that's saved demands one in its place."

"But this is the way of things," she said. "We are a warrior race."

"I know."

"And those you saved are the last of the Drang-mi-lars. Without your help today we would have been destroyed."

"I know; I'm glad of that. But I am still dumb-struck by the savagery of death. Lord Gaylor owes a debt which cannot be repaid, not in a thousand years. I cannot conceive of what he hopes to gain."

"His heart is so bereft that causing pain and death is all he can achieve. He craves the darkness because it hides his sin—"

"While we walk in the dark, as bleak and blind as him."

"We are not lost," she said, "we've merely lost a star. He has lost everything."

But Julivette's attempt to comfort me failed to

rid me of the thought that somehow I'd been sucked into Lord Gaylor's world. He desired pain and death and I'd ensured that pain and death were caused. Every action produces such profound effects, and to advance at all demands such strength of heart. It is so difficult to do right that sometimes doing wrong feels correct.

The next day we stumbled across a roadway through the dirt. Although it churned out constant noise, nothing could be seen moving along its black beam.

Angridor spoke. "This is the main highway from the deep mines in the south to the steel mills of the north," he said. "It is also a major army route to the southern testing fields, where contrivances of war are tried out on slaves. Some call it the Devil's Way; some say it is a spear produced by Gaylor's soul. It feeds several garrison towns which have been strung along its length, before eventually reaching the city of Despor. Just beyond Despor the Death Palace itself lies hidden in the hills."

"Have you ever seen the place?" I said.

"Lord Gaylor's Death Palace?" The young mage shook his head. "No, it's enwreathed by spells. The only way in or out is a protected source, a temple in Despor. We will have to barter there, or so unnerve the priests that they will reveal the door through which his dark force comes. The closer you get, the harder it becomes to see the Lord Gaylor."

"We must make haste then," grunted the Prefect Brizek, "if we have much to solve before we brave Gaylor."

The mage shrugged. "Personally, I should take my time over this. I am rather averse to death ..."

As we pierced the eerie gloom of the highway on the plain we encountered sullen throngs. Workers from the deep mines journeyed up and down, carrying on their backs baskets brimming with ore. Dressed in rags and chains, they bore the wounds and scars of Gaylor's last campaign. They were former warriors whom his armies had conquered in their last prolonged assault on the distant southern plains. Now they'd been turned to slaves destined to give their all to serve Lord Gaylor's aims.

As we joined that grim parade we offered brief salutes to the passing soldiers of Gaylor. They were travelling in convoys which cut through the crowd like phalanxes of rage, fronted by huge war-steeds, carving out thick swathes of bodies too weighed down to scramble from their path. As we were still in our captured uniforms we too appeared to be Dark Land troops, and the slaves we passed cursed every stride we took. They blamed us, with Lord Gaylor, for conquering their lands and fashioning their chains, and muttered bitterly that one day things would change and they would regain their place and turn the tide of war.

Ignoring what we heard we continued to head north, hoping to pass unchecked. We kept our heads down while our tired eyes scoured the way ahead for the frequent armed patrols which monitored the lines, and we kept our blades to hand in case they pulled us out as likely deserters. But no one challenged us, and as we trudged along we slipped into a stride which swallowed up the miles. After half a day's march we felt almost a part of those grim slaves and troops.

Even Dark Land troops require rest at the end of a hard day's march, and among the stop-over garrisons and taverns along the road we found a quiet inn. Our buying power was great, since the wearing of uniform was sufficient payment in this land, and although we proved no more popular here than we had in the mining town, the hired staff were used to showing respect, for most of them were the kin of fallen warriors and bowed to Gaylor's word.

"Some rooms, a decent meal, black polish for our boots and haircuts for the men."

The landlord bowed to Brizek and said, "It shall be done. Are you returning home from the southern plains war?"

"Do I probe your affairs?" said Brizek angrily.

"No," the landlord said, crushed.

"We are Dark Land warriors!" said Brizek. "We are not a band of horse traders fielding a herd of nags!"

"No, lord," the man whispered as he scampered out of sight to attend to our demands. We brought menace with us, we brought fear, and we let it be known.

As we chewed on a greasy meal of quarters cut from hogs, more warriors arrived. It was the Dark Land mounted lance, or at least part of it. They came in high spirits, for they had won a war and were wearing scarves and beads plucked from the latest tribe to fall beneath their spears. They came to join us, for such is the soldier's way, and promptly began to pick fights with several of our men. The tension eased slightly when Finglor ordered drinks.

"So then, you're foot-soldiers?" said a foul-skinned bear of a man who smelled worse than the food. "I couldn't stand that, travelling without a horse."

"But then we lack your skill and transparent intellect. We could not master them," Angridor said calmly, as he chewed on a bone. "We are simple foot-sloggers because we lack the wit to master basic arts like shovelling horse-dung."

"I suppose that must be true," the huge man said sagely, as he nodded at his beer. "It takes years of training to master Gaylor's steeds."

"I imagine that being short on brain cells forms a large part of the course."

"I don't think so," mused the man. "Mostly we cantered round in circles on the plain."

The man's stupidity left me almost dumbstruck and I began to wonder just how far our mage would push his luck, but I think he grew tired, because he turned away to talk to Julivette. It was left to me then to chat with the bear-like man who felt that clearing dung was something to esteem. It was with great relief that I watched him finally collapse, slain by flagons of ale.

CHAPTER 31

$\mathcal{T}$he next day we left the inn and continued on the road leading towards Despor. The previous evening, in the inn, the soldiers of the lance had been discussing Gaylor's star. It seemed it had arrived, and was safely ensconced in the Death Palace.

Our own presence in the Dark Land was a matter of some interest, as clearly Captain Broughdok had brought back news of us, and word had quickly spread that Drang-mi-laran braves were active in the land. Even worse than that, it seemed to me, was the fact that I was known to be with the Drang-mi-lars, and the word was that a youth from Moridor, by the name of Callibar, had knowledge of the Star. This made me a very valuable commodity to certain scientists of Gaylor, whose job was to destroy the Star, and a price was on my head and rough sketches of me were pasted up on walls. As with all rumours most of the truth got left behind and we were variously reported to consist of a small band of saboteurs, or a mighty tide of men in numbers so extreme we blackened half the land. I myself was a skilful Star-Adept, according to most reports; a youth of great prowess, tall, talented and strong. Not one of the reports I overheard described me as I am: a fearful, skinny youth.

"I don't know which is best," I overheard Finglor whisper to Brizek. "To continue at our slow pace, hoping to evade the guards which Gaylor has no doubt strung out along this road, or to make a determined burst to reach the Death Palace where we can end matters. The longer we take to reach it, the greater the chance that he will have destroyed the Star before we arrive, but if we raise a fuss then we are likely to be cut down before we even reach the gates."

Brizek said, "I believe we could ride through safely with little more cover than a banner of Gaylor and an authoritarian air, for I doubt that we would be stopped if we appeared to be travelling on urgent business. What the guards are looking for is a group of Drang-mi-laran warriors, not Dark Land storm-troopers, which is how we must appear. I think it would be worth the risk if it saved us several days of travel on this road." Finglor said nothing, and he continued, "You know we're doomed?"

"Probably," she murmured.

"Then what have we got to lose? Let us take our swords in our hands and ride out as we should, fighting like Drang-mi-lars."

"You are always so impetuous," she said, giving a smile. "You would ride right into Hell if you thought you would die with pride."

"You would yourself," Brizek countered. "That's why we're what we are. We two are warriors."

Brizek and several of our company returned to the wayside inn where we had spent the night. The brigade of lancers was still trapped in the torpid sleep of those who have passed a night grappling with strong beer, and I doubt they heard a sound as our men made off with their horses. It was a somewhat risky act, but as Brizek rightly said we had to reckon now in terms of hours, not days, for if Gaylor dimmed the Star all the secrecy in the world would not count for one jot. And what value have a handful of lives when the entire world teeters on the brink? Far better to die like men than grovel in the dirt like rats without a home.

*   *   *

As we cantered through the throng of slaves, the gloom appeared to be even more dense than on the night before. It was as if Lord Gaylor, in his triumph, had sent a pulse of power surging out through the land. Slaves glanced around nervously and soldiers checked their steeds, and the guards who patrolled the gloom had to squint even harder. Only our desperate band seemed conscious of the fact that this was just the beginning.

After a day's hard ride, a mighty wall appeared like a tidal wave on the plain. As we reined in our snorting horses and let them paw the ground our eyes gazed on a scene drawn from visions of Hell.

The entire land lay like a rotting corpse over which grey vultures crawled, except they were not vultures, but defeated tribes toiling to feed Gaylor. Ten thousand battered slaves clawed at the soil, and then ten thousand more, wave upon wave of them disappearing into the gloom. The only sounds we could hear were their tortured, anguished cries and the sound of whips cracked by the overseers who rode on jet-black steeds.

As we pushed our horses on, flies rose in massive swarms from bodies lying on the ground. We were still trying to follow the main route which led towards the wall, but so dense were the slaves that their numbers concealed it. All that we could see were long lines of men bent double, digging hard, not knowing why they dug. Great carts of grey dust were being wheeled away, hauled by vast lines of slaves wearing blinkers, like beasts. None guessed what it was for, and maybe it was naught but Gaylor's wicked joke, for the dirt formed great spoil-heaps which then were levelled flat, only to be rebuilt in some chaotic game. As fast as one man worked, another spilled dirt into the hole he'd dug.

"This is senseless!" I cried.

"It is Gaylor's will," said Angridor, "for he has so many slaves they don't know what to do, so they are levelling a plain around the twelve-mile walls of the city of Despor."

"This, then, is Despor?" I said.

"The grimmest town of all, a town which Gaylor built when he came to our world, a place built on the bones of those who tried to fight and those who tried to plead."

"But it appears to be burning," I said.

"That is flame-light on the walls. A ring of fire surrounds Lord Gaylor. Twenty-four hours a day, every day of the year, dead bodies feed the flames."

As Angridor finished speaking I stared up at the wall which towered above the plain, holding its ring of fire. The ring gave out a sanguine light, like blood-sick eyes gazing down at my own.

* * *

We rode through the wide main gates of the city lit by blood, and slipped down from our steeds. It proved quite impossible to move them in the press beyond the gates, and we could only stand and watch as countless slaves passed by.

"Change of watch," Angridor said. "They'll have an hour of rest while the overseers debate."

"Debate what?" I asked.

"Which mound to level next. Where to raise another heap. The overseers are trapped as surely as the slaves, but they cannot see it yet. And even if they did so I doubt they would rebel, for this entire city's a breeding ground for death. Gaylor sits in his tower and gazes on a scene created for his delight."

"The Death Palace!" I said. "It is close to where we stand?"

"Somewhere, shrouded by spells woven into thin veils. I am not sure where it is, except that it is somewhere close, hidden by temple walls."

"Which temple?" I said, leaning against the wall, for a wide phalanx of slaves was being herded past my toes.

He said, "One with black walls is as much as I have ever known. And this town is filled with temples."

Slowly the pressure eased as the slaves and guards prepared to go back to the fields. They had supped foul water and chewed on rotten bread and now, barely refreshed, were set to toil again as they would toil until they died, for such was Gaylor's wish and secret joy. The thought that he might be watching us gave me an awful chill, as if something in my stomach had just rolled onto its side and died; to suspect that the Lord of Death might be close enough to touch, if I knew where to look. I kept hunting through the faces in the crowd, as if to see a spark which would betray his disguise, but I sensed that he was far away. Gaylor had no need to soil himself by frequenting the streets when he had webs of spells which brought the streets to him. Gaylor could reach out to kill, and we would never know from whence had come the blade.

"How do we find the place?"

"The temple? We just look," the mage said with a sigh. "We must seek out the temples which are the best supplied; the ones with the best defence and a constant tide of messengers. I suspect that in the midst of them, concealed by all the rest, lies Lord Gaylor's lair. The doors to Heaven itself would prove simpler to breach, for Gaylor is no fool, and many men have tried and failed to take away his throne." So saying the mage yawned, for we had ridden hard and were sorely in need of refreshment and rest. We would require all our wits and all the strength we had to face what lay ahead.

We tethered the horses to a rail and wandered through the town with no distinct purpose. Now that we had finally arrived, the pressures of our ride seemed to have drained away much of our fire, and now that we were on the brink of finding what we had come to seek, we felt desperate for sleep. We had to summon our resources for one last brave attempt at rescuing the Star from the clutches of Gaylor, although we realized now that, so far inside his realm, such hopes were mere pipe-dreams. In fact I rather suspected that the Drang-mi-lars were secretly planning to murder Lord Gaylor as some kind of fallback plot, for without his evil lead it was doubtful that other men would dare to test the Star. Perhaps in the general confusion following his death we could concoct a plan to whisk the Star away. Or perhaps we could all sprout wings and simply glide away, the way that dreamers fly.

But even the grim soldiers who were loyal to the armies of Gaylor knew that somehow things had changed. They shared our air of despondency, for the arrival of the Star marked the beginning of the end of the world that they had known, and they must have sensed that when Gaylor had finished there would be no world at all. They must have felt as doomed as the rest of us, and yet they could not muster the strength to protest, but waited and watched, hoping they would survive whatever was to come. This meant that we were able to walk quite freely around the bleak slave-town, for no one really cared who shared those last fateful hours. Some stared up at the sky, some gazed down at the dirt, wondering if the earth would crack.

CHAPTER 32

As 'soldiers' in the town, it was harder than we thought to find somewhere to rest. Soldiers were billeted – they did not stay in inns, and questions would be asked if we tried to procure beds in barrack-huts. We wandered round forlornly, and eventually settled down outside an inn, where we took turns to drink and snatch some sleep; but we felt like hunted doves inside a nest of hawks, and were acutely scared. The longer we stayed in Despor, the more chance there was that we'd be caught, for we were bound to be spotted at some point. It only needed someone who outranked Finglor's stripes to ask the wrong question. If they asked to see our papers we might as well give in, for in a town of foes, fighting is a poor option. We had to act now – we might never again get the chance to try.

We split into three groups, each of which explored a part of the city. We checked all the temples, and most of them were black: they had black stone pillars, black walls, black steps, black roofs. They had priests dressed in black and candles made of wax which had been dyed black. We counted a hundred and twenty of them and there might have been even more, for we could not be sure that we'd spotted them all. It would be impossible to keep watch on all of them. It could take weeks to narrow down the field to the ones which we believed might lead on to Lord Gaylor, and even then we would have no guarantee that we'd picked the right one.

We needed some sort of a short cut and in the end it was our young mage Angridor who proposed a way – the mage who was my friend, or had been until that point. When I heard his suggestion I thought he must be mad.

"Give up Callibar," he said.

Bound by narrow leather thongs, I was dragged through the streets by Brizek and Finglor. "The Captain!" they cried. "The Captain of the Gate! We have arrested the youth who hails from Moridor!" To make the sham look authentic, they kept on pushing me face down into the dirt. "Where is the Captain?"

"What's going on?" men cried.

"It's the youth from Moridor! The one Lord Gaylor seeks."

"That's him?" somebody said. "He doesn't look so tough."

"We beat it out of him." Brizek dragged me forward, snarling, "Moridorian scum! He snivels like a pup and dribbles like a dog. Look at this puny youth – he is the best that Moridor could send out against Gaylor!"

With roars of laughter a large crowd gathered round and took immense delight in roughly prodding me. "A youth from Moridor – an up-world Star-Adept! He does not look too much …"

I was almost fainting as the crowd pressed all around, but at last a grim-faced man appeared, flanked by four guards. He had the sneering air and the haughty, swaggering walk of a Dark Land officer. He was in fact a Captain in the army of Gaylor, and bore the crossed-swords badge of the inner palace corps. "Get back you morons!" he sneered at the crowd huddled round our group. "We'll take over from here."

"I don't think so," said Finglor, keeping a firm grip on me. "We found this youth ourselves, so we'll take him to Lord Gaylor—"

"The heck you will," the Captain said.

"We know what Gaylor said; we've seen the wanted notices. This youth is the biggest prize after the Star itself, and we'll not yield him up."

"Do you want to go on a charge sheet?"

"I'll go to Hell itself before I'll see you claim a prize that's rightly mine. You may outrank me here, but it's no time to fight – we can all share in this."

"I claim the credit—"

"*I* claim that," Finglor said. "Though I'm prepared to grant that you played some small part. And I think Gaylor's reward will prove quite adequate to provide for all our needs. What I am offering is a peaceful end to this, for we have witnesses prepared to back us up. Look around at this crowd – I don't think they would be thrilled to see an injustice done." There was a muted murmuring from some quarters of the crowd which had clearly taken the part of the underdog, and as the Captain looked around I could see him weighing up his chances of success.

"A half share—" he said.

"A third," Finglor replied.

"Two-fifths—"

"You had nothing, and now you have a third."

"A third!" the Captain sighed.

Under the escort of the guards we were hurried through the crowd and through long, winding streets until we reached a part of town we had not explored. Here the crowd dropped back, and it was as if a shifting spell had somehow transported us to a deserted town. There was no sign of the rest of the Drang-mi-lars, who were meant to shadow us and keep us safe from harm. I could only hope that somehow Angridor would be able to detect the spell and remove it.

However, there was little time to think, for we were being hastened at some speed towards a dark temple. It was more than black. It went far beyond black. It was impenetrable.

"Wait here," the Captain said as he trotted up a flight of blood-red marble stairs to the temple loggia, where a robed priest looked down at us, eyes of ruby fire glowing from his thick black cowl. His face looked like a skull, so sunken was its flesh, so pallid its dry skin. He held a long thin prayer-necklace, and the Captain kissed the beads which trailed down to the floor. When the priest spoke his words hissed out, and his voice lanced through the air like thin tendrils of ice.

"The good Captain Belor," he said, "red-faced and flushed with fire! What brings you to our door?"

"I require immediate access to the Palace of Gaylor," the Captain said.

"On what grounds?"

"That this youth was spawned in Moridor."

"The city of the Star?"

"The very same, High-priest, and conquest of Gaylor."

"As are all obstacles—"

"Quite true, and rightly so, for none can best our lord in matters close to war."

The priest stifled a great yawn, and said, "Your point, Belor?"

"This is the Star-Adept."

This rather stunned the haughty priest, or so it at first appeared, for his slack mouth hung open and he watched me curiously. Then he said, after some thought, "This feckless mud-stained youth is an Adept of Star-lore?"

"So I believe," said Belor.

"Astonishing!" said the priest. "He looks like nothing more than a horse-tick in the dirt. Power moves in mysterious ways."

"Indeed," Belor murmured, "but can we please press on? Gaylor is extremely anxious to interrogate the youth."

"Quite so. 'Interrogate' – what a portentous word that is."

"May we proceed, High-priest, and continue with this talk at some more apt juncture? The Lord Gaylor is waiting—"

"As you wish," the priest replied, though for some time he merely stood and watched, gazing at my eyes as if to pierce my thoughts with questions of his own.

Finglor dragged me ahead without a second glance at my unhappy eyes. We were being led up the blood-red temple steps to the huge black doors of painted steel. They would withstand a siege, though that was hardly what we brought that day. All that we had was our destiny, which lay out of our hands, and the hope that Angridor could penetrate the veil which lay around this sphere of magic at the heart of the slave-town of Despor. If the young mage failed us then we would be trapped within the Death Palace of Gaylor without a hope or prayer. We would be put to death in ways so exquisite they would defy belief …

"Kneel, scum!" a guard muttered as we approached the high steel doors studded with broken skulls. "This is the final passageway to the fabled Death Palace. Kneel here and say your prayers, for all hope dies beyond."

In a tense and solemn group we all dropped to our knees and muttered our own words …

"Has the youth been checked for arms?" a hooded priest enquired as we stepped through the doors.

The Captain nodded. "He bears nothing," he said.

"And the soldiers who guard him?"

"They are similarly clear."

"And you yourself, of course …"

"My sword has long been lodged with the temple armourer. I know the routine," said Belor, "and I have been empowered to claim martial discretion when the circumstance demands. Let us cut through all this red tape and proceed straight to the veil, for time is short."

"No one goes straight through, the rule book clearly states—"

"Forget the rules, you fool!" Belor said, pushing past. "We are talking life and death, not sending through some food to feed the palace dogs." He dragged me forward, yanking me from Finglor who seemed not too distressed at having both hands free, for the time to fight was close and every second would count.

The gloom beyond the doors was lit up by the gleam of tapers set in skulls. They were like dark-red eyes glowing around the walls of a deserted black nave. The temple was nothing but a sham – an empty frame holding a veil of twisting, thick grey smoke which writhed from roof to floor.

I could scarcely believe this was the final veil which kept us from Gaylor. The trails of smoke were somewhat reminiscent of a web – maybe there was a great spider lurking within the gaseous heart of that bizarre gateway slicing through space and time. Perhaps Gaylor himself was poised to part the veil and step into the room.

"We go through two at a time, and the youth and I go first," muttered Captain Belor. "Keep close behind me." He gripped me by the arm and made me take a step towards the dense grey veil, and as he did so an arrow split the gloom and pierced his heart.

As he tumbled backwards the four guards made to turn, but each died where they stood, as did the watching priests. In the ultimate hour the tribe of Drang-mi-lar had come to our rescue.

CHAPTER 33

Finglor buckled the belt from which her long sword hung, and said, "We move as one. Forget what Belor said – we are not going through in pairs; if we're doomed to die we'll go as a band." Then she shouted, "Brizek!" for he had gone to check the dead. "You and I will lead, and take out all we can. Remember what I once said – if only one survives, make sure it's Callibar. He is the only one among us who can sabotage the Star." She turned to look at me. "Make sure you play your part. If you get near the Star you must sacrifice yourself—"

I nodded. "It shall be so."

Then we drew our swords and braced ourselves

to fight, and followed Finglor into the wall of smoke. There was a freezing blast, the scent of rain and ash, then brief oblivion.

I'm not entirely sure what I expected to find when we stepped out of the cold grey smoke. We were on a narrow pathway between steep granite banks, and the bare land round about was littered with high spurs. A lone vulture wheeled in the sky; nothing crawled on the land. It was as if all the desolation we had seen so far was no more than skirmishing in the war to kill the world, and here the war was won.

Slowly we moved forward, fanning out to right and left across the rocky path. Our swords were poised, and our archers held their bows with arrows ready notched and half-drawn back ready to fire, but nothing threatened us or tried to bar our way. The only movement we saw was rocks falling away from the steep-sided slopes like scabs leaving a sore, then tumbling down the slopes to land with dull crashes in canyons far below. The land was as empty and silent as a tomb which plunderers have ransacked aeons before. Only our scrabbling boots disturbed the scentless air.

We continued to advance as the path began to rise around a barren ridge. Some miles ahead of us, just visible through the gloom, was a mountain wreathed in clouds which writhed like angry seas, and we could see the glow of ball lightning, and hear the dull rumble of distant thunder. It was as if a mighty storm was brewing in a cauldron on a rocky peak, and as we drew closer we saw turrets arise like fingers from the cloud. This could only be the dreaded Death Palace of the fearsome Lord Gaylor, source of all the doom which filtered through this land. It seemed fitting that we approached his home to the accompaniment of storms.

A dull rain began to fall as we battled through the rocks at the foot of the black mountain. The stones grew slicker and the slopes ever more sheer, and our progress slowed, then ground to a complete standstill. It would be insane to carry on in such a deluge. We sought shelter from a rocky overhang, and crouched in numb silence while waves of rain eased past, listening to the drumming on the rock and the babbling of small streams.

We continued on our way when the rain stopped, the thunder disappeared and the ball lightning was calmed. A terrible silence hung across the world so that every tiny sound we made seemed like the crash of doom, and every stone we dislodged cavorted down the slopes with a deafening roar. We advanced like elephants, it seemed, not like the ghosts we hoped to resemble as we flitted up the slopes. The castle guards above must have looked down and wondered what was approaching.

After another hour we could make out the shapes of gargoyles on the palace towers. Gaylor's home was terrible in its silence and gloom, and the shadows on the walls seemed like effigies of doom.

Somewhere we'd missed a trail, for a wide and level track approached from the east.

"Two hours to circle the place and find an entry point," Brizek said grimly, "or we could plot an ambush somewhere along that trail and hope to intercept a supply convoy from Despor. Deceiving the guards who man the gates could prove a difficult task, for if we assault them we give ourselves away, and if we try to talk we might as well give up. That said, I doubt those walls will be riddled with holes through which we could enter." The Prefect ran his hands through his lank hair. We were so close to Gaylor's lair that we could reach out and touch its walls, yet we could not pass its gate. It was a bizarre situation: we could not advance but there would be little sense in retracing our steps.

I said, "The sewer ducts – could we not pass through there?"

"They will be safely barred," Brizek said, "and

doubtless bound with spells. I doubt that even rats climb into Gaylor's home and live to tell the tale. The man is clearly some kind of magician as well as a thief and the kind of dictator who does not know when to stop. Our only chance might be to lure him out, though I doubt he'd be fool enough to walk out of his own safe halls."

While the Prefect was talking to us our sentries heard the sounds of movement on the trail, and came back to report. One said, "A brigade of troops and archers has drawn up. I think that they know we are here."

There comes a time to fight, and a time to recognize when one has lost a war. How long the palace guards had been aware of our presence it was impossible to say, but probably ever since we had passed through the temple gate. They had let us sweat and toil and clamber up the slopes, then quietly surrounded us. There was very little we could do about it, for we were only thirty strong and a forest of arrows was pointing at our hearts. Unless we chose to die out there on the trail, we had to yield our swords.

"A very proper move," said the Captain of the Guard as Finglor sheathed her blade. "Death is a messy business when it is conducted in the raw. It would be such a waste when we have much better ways inside the Death Palace. Even though your quest has failed, you did advance much further than we would once have believed, so at least you go out with pride." Laughing, he unclipped Finglor's sword and tossed it to a guard who stood some yards behind. "To think that it all ends like this!" he said. "So much effort for no reward."

"Wait here," the Captain said as we shivered in heavy rain in a courtyard lined with black stone. Our wrists were bound and ropes were looped round our necks, but we could still raise our eyes to gaze on Gaylor's halls, and what we saw was death. The murals painted on the walls showed tortures and agony; we could half-hear the screams of victims, we could taste their blood, we could scent their torment with every breath we took. We had arrived in that place beyond all hope: Lord Gaylor's Death Palace.

"The youth from Moridor, who is called Callibar, will take a step forward."

The Captain waited while we stood in silent rows, then I stepped forward. I knew that if I did not do so, the troops would begin to kill the Drang-mi-lars and would continue murdering our band until but three remained: the youthful Angridor, Julivette and myself. Then they'd kill Julivette, since she was quite obviously not the bearer of my name.

"The rest of you wait here."

The Captain took my arm and led me through a door.

CHAPTER 34

I had pondered long and hard on the feelings I might have should I meet the 'Lord of Death'. I had dreamed that he might destroy me with a quick glance from his eyes or take my quaking soul and squeeze it in his palms, or peel out every nerve and sinew I possessed and weave them into string. But in the event he was not like that, and in fact was so different from my imaginings that for a moment I thought I had been shown into the presence of someone who merely served Gaylor.

"Sit over there," he said, gesturing with a quill which was blackened with ink. "I shall be with you shortly, but I must first attend to this." He returned to a crumpled chart which was held open by mugs. Beyond the small table on which the chart was spread stood a grey, withered mage. "I need some kind of earthquake, or something of that ilk," he said to the mage.

"It can't be done, my lord; it has been tried before."

"And what was the result?"

"The mage who cast the spell was sucked into the ground."

"By a massive earthquake?" the Lord Gaylor enquired.

"By a demon from the earth."

"I see." Lord Gaylor sighed. He fiddled with the parchment chart, and dropped a blob of ink from the pen onto his cape. "Have you tried others, though?"

"No, lord."

"Then test one now. In fact, pick out six mages and let them all try. Bring the results to me if they look at all hopeful."

"Yes, lord," the mage replied.

"And bring me some conquests – I grow bored with doing all the work of killing worlds myself."

"We could help with the Star—"

"No, keep away from the Star. The Star is my affair." Then Lord Gaylor straightened and turned to look at me, dismissing the ancient mage with a simple, terse command, and the dark flames in his eyes blossomed into a blaze which all but engulfed me.

"So you are Callibar," murmured the elegant Lord of Death as he lowered himself onto a throne. The court room was empty now but for us two, and not a single guard or slave was anywhere in sight. If I had been better prepared or possessed of more courage I could have strangled him, for he was so close to me that I could reach out to touch his cape, could map every line of his slim, fine-featured face, could gaze into those deep blue eyes which once witnessed the death of half a world.

"Are you a Star-Adept?"

"No, Lord," I said softly.

"I did not think you were." Lord Gaylor gave a very soft sigh. "You are too simple for that, not ravelled by the woes of tending the Star, not yet devoured inside by the cancer of its light, which eats away at bones." He tapped his fingers. "Do you know it's killing you?"

"Yes, Lord."

"As it kills us all by a destructive force swifter than thought. It kills life and hope and eats away our wills, until only flesh remains."

"But, Lord, it's God-sent."

"God has sent many things, and most of them are dangerous or at best double-edged. What your God sends with one hand is snatched away by the other – that's how a balance is kept. Your God seduces you and wraps you in fear so that all you believe is what He makes appear. Your God is like a child who cries when it's happy or laughs when it is sad."

I said, "You lose me, Lord—"

"I've read your 'Words of God'. I've heard the sacred creeds to which you all pay lip-service. Yours is a jealous God."

I wandered in a maze of shrubs carved out of rust-flecked stone, while Gaylor plotted war. The Lord of Death was trying to persuade me to help him break the Star, for he admitted that he had not the power. He said that everything he had done was for the love of Man and anguish for the world. He said that we were destroying the world through petty wars and strife, while we had so much to give and so much hope to bring.

Gaylor said that we had been blinded by the misdeeds of a God so jealous in Himself that He could never rest, but would bring down plagues and wars, and sacrifice the world in order to keep us in His flock.

At times all of this grew fairly complex, but what I think the Lord of Death meant was that our only hope was to begin afresh, to wipe out all mistakes and build the world anew, working from what we'd learned.

"What do you see out there?"

"I see a destroyed world."

"I see an empty page."

We were standing on a high rock overlooking an empty plain where storm winds gathered dust to cover up the land. To north and south, to east and west, lay nothing but desert. Nothing was moving but the dust motes in the wind, and nothing grew from the plain but towers of blasted rock. Nothing flew through the sky; nothing crawled on the land. I had seen all this before.

Gaylor said, "There is so much potential for fashioning a world freed from the fears of men, so much free spirit that we need merely tame; so much time and such space in which to start from scratch. If we just take a seed and nourish it with love—"

"And you're the seed?" I asked.

To my surprise the Lord of Death snorted. "I am too corrupt," he said, "too tainted by the pain and misery I've caused, too cursed by my own sins and burdened by the lives trampled beneath my horses' hooves. For am I not the very Devil incarnate?" he shouted to the wind. "Have you not heard my name spoke in impious tones?"

He gave a laugh. "The Devil. They're fools to think I have such power."

CHAPTER 35

While Lord Gaylor worked and talked I wandered through the halls of his grim Palace of Death. I was given an absolute freedom to go wherever I chose, and no one intervened or closed any doors to me. The only room to which I was denied access was the Sanctum of the Star. Even Lord Gaylor's private apartments were not beyond my range, and I would often slip inside when I was searching for rest, but in the main I simply roamed, unhindered and unsung, for several confused days.

"So, Cal," Lord Gaylor said as I stared across his realm from an embrasure in a tower, "how are your spirits now?"

"Bemused," I said softly. "Lost in the Gordian knots which form your grand designs. Confused by being allowed to wander as I will through your private domain. Why do you not just torture me, as you no doubt did my friends? Why invest so much time and precious effort in prising out what I know? Why not just rip it out, and find what little worth there is in my knowledge?" I turned to look at him. "What do you hope to prove? That you can seduce my soul into the Dark Land's ways?"

Lord Gaylor smiled at me. "You think too much," he said. "And you are hunting for something which is not really there, for such plans as I possess are not nearly as grand as you'd like to believe. I am a simple wanderer in the world, much like yourself, and maybe that's the spark which I sensed when I met you, for we have so much in common, so many hopes and dreams; we are so thoughtful, Cal." He smoothed his flowing cloak, and continued, "And that's rare, for so many men these days smother their thoughts with cares."

I said, "My friends, Lord—"

He said, "Your friends are safe. They are in the town, where they are well cared for. Unlike you, Callibar, they would have killed me first and wondered afterwards."

* * *

I continued to listen to the words of Lord Gaylor, as I sat in the window in the tower. He stood next to me, staring across the plains, and the whispers of his cloak formed a soothing backdrop to the gentle, sombre tones in which he outlined his plans. I knew that he was trying to win me over so that I would willingly assist him in his quest to dim the precious light of the last threatening star, and there were times when he came close to promising me power over his new, dark universe.

"My talk of God", he said, "is not just idle talk, but comes from deep inside. For ever since I was a small child I have wondered at the world, and pondered how it is that it all turned out so wrong. I dreamed that, given time, it would be possible to unite all mankind."

"By killing it?" I said.

"Conquest is but a minor part of a much larger design," murmured the Lord Gaylor. "For sometimes men are blind, and sometimes their own words drown out what they should hear. You must look beyond that to see what can be done, and how being cruel can sometimes be a kindness. If I could form one world, with all men beneath one flag, old rivalries would die. All the hatred and anger of the past would wither like a worm deprived of food and light, and we could build a world of majesty and power where mankind could forge ahead. There would be no more resentments and picking at old wounds. No more would men be afraid to raise their heads. All men would be born the same, one nation under God—"

"And who'd be God?" I said.

The Lord of Death grew bored with trying to win me round and resorted instead to veiled threats. He said, "I could force you, Cal—"

"I have never doubted that."

"But then you would rather die than tell me what you know."

"I don't know very much," I said, staring at him across the table. We were having breakfast when he tried this new tack, and the gloom which filled the room was echoed in his eyes. The meat on which I chewed felt brittle as rock, and almost crushed my teeth.

"Why are you so reluctant," he asked, "to take my side? To grant that I could be right and others wrong?"

"Because the ones I know, who would die opposing you, are not called the 'Lord of Death'."

"It's a stupid title!" he said, dismissing it with a wave of a slim, elegant hand. "It is nothing but a phrase thought up by simple minds envious of my power."

I said, "But you've killed them; you've killed off half the world!"

He said, "Somebody has to die if things are

going to change, and I am growing restless!" He pounded with his fist, and I froze in mid-mouthful as his eyes blazed into mine. "I can compel you, Cal!"

"I am not afraid to die."

"It is not you who will die, for I have the Drang-mi-larans imprisoned in my cells, and every one of them will die to test your fool resolve. I shall take the fairest first, the young girl Julivette, and tear out both her eyes. I shall have her *eat* them before I'll let her die—"

The tension in the air was tangible. Lord Gaylor had gone to war and I had a poor defence, for I could not watch my friends die.

"What do you wish to know?" I asked as Gaylor's deep blue eyes gazed coldly at my own.

He said, "The Star-shielding – it has begun to crack as if the leaden plates are dissolving from within, and nothing I try seems to hinder the rate of the metal's decay. Even the iron cart beneath it is now glowing like a lamp—"

I said, "The Star is still on it?"

"I daren't risk moving it. I am not ashamed to say that it is quite possible I have misjudged your Star. I sense some irony in the fact that men prostrate themselves before me while this strange, glowing rock resists me to its core, and the more I attempt, the stronger it becomes in its rebuffs. I suspect that its power is far greater than I at first assumed. I have great respect for the members of your guild. Their power must be awesome—"

"The Star was sent by God, and it will not react well to the probings of the Dark."

"But it is just a star, a glowing lump of rock; it has no character. What you are suggesting is a 'personality', but the Star has no desires and no conscious train of thought. It is pointless to attempt to muddle my thoughts with ancient Star-mystique."

"I would not do that," I said, "but the Star does resist all men, and the Adepts do use spells to keep it in check. It takes years to learn these spells, and we do not have the means to learn them here, even if we could."

"What about tungsten?"

"It's possible," I replied. "Long, thin restraining bands may hold the shield in place. Tungsten has a high melting-point—"

"Though even that will fail and part eventually. What is required is some breathing space: a temporary lull from the constant surge of power which the Star is emitting. I need to find more time, to seek out a different route."

"Then bury it," I said.

I had to hold my breath as I tried my desperate ploy to keep the Star intact. If I allowed Lord

Gaylor to destroy it then there would be no hope left, and all life on this world would trudge through an endless gloom. While the Star survived, a new promise might emerge from some quiet corner. Star-light would become a symbol for all who fear the dark, and those with enough heart might move to seek it out. Some day they might break the chains of Gaylor, the Lord of Death, and snatch back their future.

"How should I bury it?" he asked, his eyes like blue-tinged flames simmering in his fine face.

I said, "Inside a canyon, or a mine shaft underground. Somewhere so dark and deep that none will interfere. Wrap it around with spells, drive them into the rock, build an impenetrable wall. The earth will cushion it while you search for the means to banish it for good and cleanse the world of it."

He said, "For your sake, Cal, I hope your words are wise, or you are the first to die."

CHAPTER 36

Once again I held my breath, though this time not from fear but from anticipation. One thing had always had been denied to me during the years in which I toiled as a novice in the guild which brought Moridor its starlight: I had never seen the Star. I had been quite close to it, and I had even glimpsed its shield, but the next time Lord Gaylor went to the Sanctum of the Star I would accompany him. I would wear a leaden shield-cloak, and a mask to guard my eyes. I would don the steel gauntlets which would help preserve my hands. I would stand at his side as Lord Gaylor gauged the cracks, and I would offer my advice.

"What do you think the chances are of us surviving if we fail?"

I said, "I have never been there, and so cannot reply, and no one in my lifetime has ever seen the Star's full power revealed, but I know that even Star-Adepts receive only small glimpses; small fractions of small parts. Future-lore is therefore speculation, but I believe it suggests that the Star's untrammelled light beams would blast through rock and flesh. They are so strong that tunnels would be burned through the very earth."

"So we would probably not live for too long?" Gaylor said ironically.

"The lore suggests for less than one heartbeat," I said. "Our flesh would vaporize; our bones would turn to dust; we would fade on the breeze."

"A cheerful prospect for the Lord of Death himself," murmured the Lord Gaylor as he stared out on the plains. "All my darkness ends and all that I've worked for dies, and all for this one risk."

That was a strangely pregnant moment which we shared on the palace battlements, where we watched hungry grey hawks circling overhead, for I sensed that the Lord of Death had come close to admitting to me what it was that he most feared. It was neither torment nor death which he abhorred, nor the loss of his own tortured soul, which had vanished years before. I believe that what Lord Gaylor feared, over and above all things, was to find his soul again.

"Come, Callibar," he said as he tossed back his

long black cloak, "our time is running short. And the whole grey world is waiting to see how Gaylor fares in his final, great battle to undermine a star. It waits to see who will win, the darkness or the light."

I trailed the Lord Gaylor through the long and twisting ways of his strange Palace of Death. We walked through a profound darkness, for it seemed the stones themselves actually devoured light, and the small lanterns on the walls had little more effect than that of glow worms in a storm. Although I had been in the palace for sixteen days, and had grown somewhat used to things, I felt the darkness change that day. It was as if the essence of Lord Gaylor's brooding thoughts was captured by the walls and thrown back. Trapped in his own grim world, Gaylor let darkness play.

Narrow spiral stairwells led us onwards and down into the building's heart. At each new level the aura of the place grew ever more intense and its silence more severe, and the cold-eyed palace guards, stationed at every turn, appeared more statue than man.

I hurried to keep pace with the fleet-footed Lord Gaylor as he raced through a long, silent hall. "It will be too late tomorrow," he murmured, glancing up at an oil painting on a wall, which depicted him on horseback. "It is too late to kill a star when the star has already killed you. It is too late by far." Never before had the Lord of Death spoken in such a way; never before had he confessed to having doubts. His flowing cloak rustled with a sound like desperate prayer as its hem trailed on the earth.

"My Lord?" I said.

"What is it, youth?"

"Are you afraid today?"

"Nothing makes me afraid." Lord Gaylor turned to look at me, and seemed surprised that I should dare to ask a question such as this. He said, "The shielding fails and will collapse within twelve hours. I am preoccupied." Then he turned away again and, sweeping up his cloak, strode off into the gloom. He kept glancing around, as if to chivvy me to match his storming pace.

Down and down, spiralling round and round, we headed underground. I grew increasingly nervous as the final rooms approached and the presence of the Star made itself more apparent. Static charge filled the air, and strengthened rapidly to near fever pitch. Having never before experienced this I said, "The Star goes wild!"

"It throbs with such a power that it threatens to erupt," Gaylor said.

I cried, "It is God's rage!"

He said, "Forget God's rage. There are no gods down here." He took up a heavy shield-cloak and flung it at my feet, saying, "Put on your cloak and find yourself a mask. You have waited all your life to draw close to your great Star, and now your hour arrives."

Lord Gaylor beat on a massive steel drum to warn the guards within that we would very soon enter the Chamber of the Star, and I fumbled with my clothes, straining to strip them off with fingers stiff with fear.

In a darkness so complete that I was worse than blind, I listened. I could hear the sound of my own pulse hammering in my ears, and the whispers of my hair against the mask's lining. I could feel my pounding heart and the crushing weight of the leaden cloak pressing down on my shoulders.

I was barely able to move now, so heavy was the mask, so ponderous my limbs in the thick, protective cloak. The heat my body produced had no means to escape, and my tense back streamed with sweat.

"Four minutes!" cried a guard.

With a rumble of heavy steel and a great clanking of chains the Chamber door was raised. I had my eyes closed, and my fists clenched so tightly that I could feel warm blood trickling down my palms.

The breaths which filled my lungs were so rapid that my blood began to race. My fingers tingled and stars burst in my brain like a firework display across a midnight sky.

Then the Lord of Death touched my arm to guide me through the doors.

Never in my small and fragile life would I have known how brilliant is the Star if it were not for the Lord Gaylor. I had to grip his shoulder as my instincts urged me back, shocked by the force of light which filled the Chamber, for even through the mask the Star was like several suns condensed into one. It shone like the birth-smile of a god. It shone like life and hope, and mountains set on fire. It shone so brightly it hurt, as if the beams were plunging straight into my soul.

For several stunned moments I stood and watched then, as my thoughts recovered, I felt great waves of heat. They were lancing through the room, causing my cloak to glow, charring the cloth beneath. And what most astonished me was that all this glory came while the Star was still contained inside its spell-blessed dome. What a force would be unleashed if the Star's shielding collapsed, and the light was set free!

"You see the cracks?" Lord Gaylor asked.

I nodded.

"They were caused on the journey through

Dark Land. I think the jarring—"

"The shield always has cracks. Most of the Adepts' work consists of patching it up. But without their spells and the knowledge of how they work, there is not much we can do. You will certainly have to move the Star to a safer place, for if the shield fails here all life will be destroyed. Light will burn through the walls of your entire Death Palace, indeed this whole mountain."

"Should we try with tungsten?"

"On a nickel-ferrous base. A temporary bond is all that is required. And reinforce the cart, for it will not stand the strain of being driven again."

Even as I spoke my last words soldiers encased in lead were rushing to respond to the Lord Gaylor's commands. They strained to brace the dome, handling it delicately like an egg, watching their gauntlets steam.

The heat was so intense that Lord Gaylor and I retreated from the room. We went to a nearby chamber where we struggled out of our cloaks and Gaylor offered me lumps of ice with which to soothe my skin. He showed me to a chair which, even at this range, felt warm from the Star's heat.

He said, "If I am successful, darkness will rule the world and all stars in the sky will one day be put out."

I said, "God will punish you, I feel. He will not permit it."

"But what will He do to me, do you think, Callibar?" asked Gaylor, and I could sense the irony in his voice.

"I don't know yet," I said, "but I know that God's revenge will be a mighty force."

Then Lord Gaylor ruffled up my hair almost tenderly, smiling at my taut face. He said, "The Lord of Death and your God of light. What a debate we'll make!"

CHAPTER 37

*T*welve black horses draped with lead were brought from the stables of the grim Death Palace. Though the beasts skittered fretfully they were harnessed to the cart and, taking up the slack, began to haul it through the Palace doors. With blinkers to shield their eyes they followed in the wake of Gaylor's beast-master. The man was carrying a fuming lantern on which the horses fixed their gaze as if it were a charm to keep them safe from harm. Lord Gaylor and I were seated on the cart. I felt in need of charms too.

Boom! Boom! Two mighty timpani announced that we were coming.

Sentries threw open steel doors and cleared a path for us. The entire Death Palace was put on full alert. Nothing – no stone, no rat, no unexpected draught – must interfere with the cart. The cart thundered as it trundled up the wide, gently-sloping passageway leading to the gates. Thunder came from its wheels, thunder bounced from the walls, thunder beat in my heart.

Boom! Boom! Again the drums sounded, and again the waiting guards leapt to clear our path.

Flickering lanterns cast shadows over us. The leather harnesses of the horses creaked and strained. A rich and earthy smell rose from the horses' flanks and their hooves struck sparks.

I checked behind me to see that the Star was safe, and sensed great waves of power pounding against the bonds. Huge chains held it in place, keeping it secure on the long iron cart.

"Release the outer gates!" Lord Gaylor yelled ahead as the cart crept from the gloom.

We emerged into the empty courtyard through which I had first arrived, where murals depicted scenes of death, and gargoyles gazed down with sullen eyes, dripping with black-stained tears. A large contingent of armoured cavalry was waiting by the gates to form the Star-escort. They fell in on either side of us and more riders took the rear, so that we were protected all round.

*   *   *

Enormous steel gates creaked and slowly opened wide. Beyond lay a desolate landscape of great gullies choked with rocks, dry stream beds, swirling cloud. Grey hawks flew overhead on this roof of the world, where Gaylor had his home. Slowly the Star-cart rumbled through the gates like a harbinger of doom, bringing its message from the gods. The message said that this day would be a day of death for half the living world.

CHAPTER 38

oom! Boom! The riders up ahead warned of the Star's approach.

The cart moved along a steep and wide track which curved around the flanks of the Mountain of Gaylor, heading for the low-slung hills. The hills were pitted with craters made when Gaylor tested his guns of war, and he planned to bury the sacred Star inside the deepest pit, in a hole which scarred the ground for a thousand yards or more around. He would shield the pit with layers of shale and rock, and set spells over it, then he would experiment with ways to dim the Star for good. And when he knew how to do this, he would return to the Star and blast it from the world.

We trundled down the track, guiding the weighty cart. Close-ranked beside us came the Escort of the Star, equipped with flaming brands to light the road ahead. The jangling of their spurs and the creaking of their girths was the only sound to be heard apart from the rumbling of the iron cart, which made the very earth vibrate beneath its wheels. It was a strange parade that our group made that day: darkness enriched by flame.

"It may take several hours," said Gaylor as the cart crept slowly down the track. Although I heard him I offered no response, for my thoughts were up ahead, fixed on the beast-master. The man was looking up as if he could see something, staring at the southern skyline, where a thin haze lay over the spires and towers of the city of Despor. Although we were entirely lost to the towns-people, they were quite visible to our un-enchanted eyes, and we could ride down into the town of death whenever we chose to do so.

"What's that man looking at?" I heard the Lord Gaylor ask as the beast-master halted in his stride. "What are you looking at?" he cried, and the man turned round.

"I thought I saw something flash in the

southern sky," he said. "I thought I heard some-thing – a thrumming in the air—"

The cart had stopped now, and Lord Gaylor stood erect, peering back through the gloom towards the distant town. "I can't hear anything," he said. But he could sense something; we all could sense something. Some kind of 'presence' was forming in the air; and a burst of static charge flickered across the sky. Someone was wielding a spell designed to cut through the veils which Gaylor had put up.

"A witch spell!" cried Gaylor as a spark of light broke through the southern sky. "It is the witch-queen Mandrigor! She's coming back again!" He snatched the horses' reins and gave his whip a crack. "I thought she'd been destroyed, but the old crone lingers on, determined to best me!"

As Lord Gaylor bent to his whip the horses bucked and reared, and the Star-cart gave a lurch, then thundered down the track. Horses and men scattered as the Lord of Death himself caught a glimpse of his ultimate fear.

CHAPTER 39

She came out of the southern sky on a horse dripping with flame, which set light to the sky. She came with thunder and lightning in her hands, she came with fire and wrath bursting from her quiver, and as she aimed her golden bow, crimson flares shot out, blazing towards the earth. The ground exploded to both sides of the track. Terrified horses reared, throwing men from their backs. The panicked beast-master ran in front of the cart and was trampled to death.

And for the first time, I saw Lord Gaylor scared; I saw the colour drain from his tense, startled face.

I had never known before how potent was the witch, how great her power.

* * *

The cart which bore the Star clattered across the earth towards the waiting pit. Galloping flat out around us were the riders on black steeds, who seemed to be bearing the brunt of Mandrigor's attack. Time and again, bursts of lightning struck them from their mounts. They were screaming and levelling their spears, but there was nothing they could fight against. For the witch sped here and there through the sky, touching and destroying men and drifting away again.

"I'll see that witch in Hell!" I heard Lord Gaylor snarl as he lashed out at the horses. "I once destroyed her, or so it at first appeared. She must have crawled away and hidden in the rocks. Now, like a poisoned worm, she turns and tries to take my prize! But I'm the Lord Gaylor, the Lord of Death himself! Nothing stands in my way; nothing thwarts my command!"

He raised the stinging whip and, with a mighty crash, brought it down on a horse.

Through darkness lit by flame and silence split by roars, Lord Gaylor drove the cart.

The witch was hunting us across the base of a wide, flat valley which led towards the hills. She had brought her horse to the ground and it sprinted after us, dripping trails of flame.

Gaylor's soldiers rallied as they saw the horse touch down. They saw that there was no longer any fire in the witch's empty quiver. Then they saw Mandrigor toss her bow aside, take hold of her sword, and head straight for them. And in a great explosion of bodies, light and steel she hurtled through their ranks and bore down on the cart. I saw Lord Gaylor turn to check on her advance, and I kicked him aside.

Grabbing the flapping reins I tried to steer the horses away from the approaching pit. I heaved them sideways, but the black beasts thundered on, racing towards their doom. I screamed every command I'd heard, and they just shrugged them off. For the beasts had been driven insane by the terror all around and nothing could slow their charge. They had but one desire: to outrun the grey horse which came dripping with flames.

"Move over, Callibar," the witch said as she leapt from her horse onto the cart. "This is not your time. It is the time for me to settle an old grudge that's brewed for seven years." Then Mandrigor took the long reins and wrapped them around her arm, leaning back in the cart until every muscle screamed. And the pounding beasts slowed down and began to turn slowly back towards Despor.

CHAPTER 40

We exploded through the veil of smoke which served as Gaylor's gate inside the black temple. Startled priests scattered as the cart tore down the aisle, sparks shooting from the wheels and fumes leaking from the Star. Men in black hoods froze, statue-like, in our path and were trampled aside.

I saw the High Priest pick up a crimson sword and leap to bar our way, but with a wave of her flame-drenched hand the witch turned him to smoke, and the Star cart thundered on.

We clattered through the doors, hurtling across the steps and on into the town. All veils of secrecy were shattered in our wake, all things once concealed became clear to the gaze, and the people of Despor gazed in shocked amazement at Gaylor's Death Palace brooding amongst the peaks which towered above their city.

We continued to hurtle through the crowds, scraping sparks from walls with the iron sides of the cart, and there was barely room for men to scatter from our path.

"They're coming now," I said as, glancing behind me, I saw signs of pursuit. "Men on black horses are pouring through the breach. The riders of Gaylor are forming strike-waves in the streets—"

"And the soldiers up ahead are trying to bar our way with barricades of steel." The witch laughed crazily. "But we will take them all on! We will take this sacred Star far from the grim Gaylor. We'll cut them down like chaff, we'll strike them from the earth!" And an arrow pierced her throat …

"Ye gods," Mandrigor gasped as she slumped down at my feet, and let the long reins fall. "Some fool has shot me!" She forced a desperate laugh. "The great witch Mandrigor felled by a single shaft. You will have to take the reins – continue through the gates and head towards the west."

I said, "No, eastward – we must ride for Moridor!"

"Your town is long gone," she said. "Gaylor had

it destroyed. Ride hard towards the west, head for the hills and pray that I don't die."

Then the witch fell backwards, and I tried to keep her safe while steering for the gates and wrestling with the reins. And a voice inside my head cried, '*My home has been destroyed!*' as troops closed in around us.

CHAPTER 41

We thundered through the gates with hardly less impact than a cart from Hell itself. Stunned sentries fell back as we burst from Despor's gloom, and the shocked guards of the watch had no chance to respond. They had hauled out spiked hurdles in an attempt to slow our flight, but the horses crashed through them, protected from them and from the arrows which hurtled down by their leaden trappings. While the guards stared in dismay we left Despor behind and galloped down the road.

With every passing moment, however, the servants of Gaylor regained their misplaced wits and snatched up spears and swords, and by the time we reached the fields a tide of men was streaming after us. Men came on horseback, on foot, by ox-drawn cart; men came with lance and bow, and the war-tools of Gaylor. When I glanced back I saw a whole army of troops pursuing us.

On and on the Dark Land soldiers came, fanning out claw-like, racing across the fields in a long, uneven line of horses, arms and flags. The slaves toiling on the land fled from their path, but many were trampled underfoot. I saw some raise their hoes and try to defend themselves. I myself ran some of them down, for it was impossible to steer the charging cart. I could only let it follow the tracks which cut across the fields towards the western hills.

Boom! Boom! Once more I heard the thud of pounding drums, this time in the east. As I risked a quick glance in the direction of the sound I saw a line of men march out of the Dark Land gloom. They bore tools which they held like arms – hammers, axes and staves – and strode beneath plain flags.

"Mandrigor!" I hissed.

She said, "The mining town has come to face Gaylor."

Boom! Boom! The miners' drums thundered across the plain which lies before Despor, and as I watched in horror, massed ranks of Gaylor's troops fell on the men, and the brave souls who hew black rock took on the blades and shields of those whose work is war.

Yet though clearly outnumbered and badly equipped, the miners did not flinch but battled fiercely, grappling with the troops, hauling down stray lancers and charging cavalry.

They took on their foes with all the savagery and fury of a race long held in thrall to the wishes of Gaylor, picking up fallen swords and wading into the ranks of Gaylor's front-line troops. They fought them for every inch of ground, tracking troops through the fields and forcing them to the walls. They fought tooth and nail, carving a swathe of death across Lord Gaylor's dirt.

As I rode I witnessed immense bravery and tragedy. I heard shouts of pride and screams from those near death and I breathed the wretched stink of war. Although most of the men died, they had gained me precious time.

CHAPTER 42

I urged the tiring beasts to tackle the rock-strewn slope of the first lonely hill. Mandrigor had said that was where I should go, and I hoped that she had reserves of miners in the hills, waiting to guard the Star. I hoped they would shield me and escort me, but when I looked around I could see no one, just empty hills, barren as tide-washed rocks.

I had ridden into a death-trap, which was no place to make a stand against the rampant hordes of Lord Gaylor's Dark Land troops.

And the troops were coming now, leaving death in the fields like so much trampled wheat.

We were almost at the summit of the hill when the

horses offered up the last of their efforts. They were snorting horribly as I wedged the wheels with rocks and helped the failing witch to clamber from the cart. "Death strikes my heart," she said, "but I have one last wish – to see Lord Gaylor's face."

I said, "He will kill you—"

"I am already dead," Mandrigor said. "I died when Lord Gaylor over-ran Dark Land. I died a little each time he spoke, each time he blinked his eye; each time he raised his hand. The Lord of Death is a cancer, and I shall watch him die before I leave this earth for realms he cannot command. I shall die watching him weep, knowing how great is fear, how pitiless his end."

I said, "But Lord Gaylor's soldiers already circle the hill. We have no place to go, and no rescue is at hand."

"Give Gaylor what he wants," she said. "Give him the Star."

Then the witch died in my arms.

CHAPTER 43

The death of Mandrigor seemed like the final note in the symphony I had played. There would be no encore, for I had adventured all I could, and that bare, lonely hill would witness my sad end. For without the horses I could no longer transport the Star, and their strength was spent. They lay sprawled out on the ground, barely able to move even the muscles of their eyes as I crouched down to unhook the straps which bound them to the cart.

And then I simply stood my ground, for there was nowhere else to go, and no brave comrades appeared to shield me from my doom. But while the Dark Land soldiers formed long black lines round the hill, I stood guard over the witch.

Death must come to all of us, it is said, and I am no exception. I watched it approach gradually, as I gazed at the black horses riding across the plain, bearing men whose hearts were filled with the shadows cast by the cloak of the Lord of Death. And on a huge grey charger whose spirit had been forged in the deepest fires of Hell, the Lord Gaylor himself picked his way through the fields, trampling on the dead.

Boom! Boom! This time the sound of the slow and deep drumbeat was the thunder in my heart.

CHAPTER 44

At the base of the bare grey hill on which I stood alone, Lord Gaylor reined in his steed. "Callibar!" he cried. "There is a time to fight, a time to run and hide and a time to die. I'm glad you are not so brave that you waste your time waging a pointless fight. Your friends lie slaughtered or rotting in my gaols. Your only hope, the witch, now wanders through limbo. You have no sword to raise, nor can you trust in prayer. Descend to face your doom!"

Then, like a father reaching out to his son, Lord Gaylor offered his hand as if to take my own, and I saw all the gloom and hopelessness which festered in his soul.

For he was dead inside, as dead as the grey chunks of rock which wedged the Star-cart's wheels and trapped it on the slope. With an empty heart I walked back towards the cart and kicked those chunks away....

Hell thundered from the wheels as the carriage gathered speed and hurtled down the slope. Horrified stormtroopers broke ranks as it bounced off the rocks, tearing ferocious strips from the dust-dry arid earth. The panic in their eyes was mirrored by the fear which I sensed in my own.

The Lord of Death screamed at me from the path of his approaching doom ... for the Star was working loose, its bonds torn apart by the jolting of the cart.

"You'll destroy all of us!" he screamed. "You'll damn your soul!"

But the Star-cart thundered on to grind him in the dirt; and as it collided with a rock, its shielding burst apart.

For one long, stunned moment the whole of Dark Land froze, then waves of fire scorched us. I was flung backwards by the anger of a star which had for so long brewed inside its lead-bound shield as veil upon veil of light dispersed across the fields and leapt through the hills. And in that instant I realized the true purpose of the Star, and how wronged it had been. It was not meant for Moridor; it was not meant to be caged; it was for everyone.

CHAPTER 45

I lost track of the hours I wandered blind, blasted by hot, dry wind. I do not know if I wandered north or south, east or west. I wandered like a child, stumbled like an old man. I advanced on my knees across fields, rocks and streams, and I cried at every step.

For the Star had cheated me by burning out my sight. It tore loose half my skin, it seared my brain, and turned my thoughts to ash. It left me half-dead inside.

"Callibar?"

"What?" I said, as Gaylor's chatelain approached me from behind.

"Lord Gaylor lies crushed beneath the cart," he said. "His darkness leaves this land as light bleeds from the Star."

I had to force a laugh at the grim irony which had left my own eyes blind. Yet I sensed that justice, or something resembling justice, had been done. I turned to grip the man's arm. I said, "He's truly dead?"

EPILOGUE

Like clear skies after rain, my vision at last returned to me. Not the same vision, though – my sight was tinged with blood, as if all Dark Land's pain had seeped into my soul; as if I'd always take death with me. I'd carry memories of miners who had died. I'd remember Bakkmalar, whose loss had helped me survive. I'd remember the witch who'd died in my arms, believing she had failed.

But I've a question now that's haunted me a while. What name do you give to one who will not die? What do you call the youth who fights down Death itself?

Some call me *'Lord of Life'*.

* * *

The Lord of Life returned to the surface world with his small band of friends.

It was a long trek, but we weren't short of time. In fact, we had not much else now that our great quest was over. We had time to check our lives, to look back and then ahead, wondering what was to come.

What will be waiting there, now Gaylor's smoke has cleared? What chance will the world take, now chances have been bought?

How will I fit back into Moridor, my home?

Maybe I'll ride on by ...